Losii
Arianna

Losing Arianna

Mairi Speirs

Elephant
Chance

Published in 2023 by Elephant Chance

Copyright © 2023 Mairi Speirs

Mairi Speirs has asserted her right to be identified as the author of this
Work in accordance with the Copyright, Designs and Patents Act 1988

ISBN Paperback: 978-1-9164541-2-5
Ebook: 978-1-9164541-3-2

A CIP catalogue copy of this book can be found in the British Library.

Published with the help of Indie Authors World
www.indieauthorsworld.com

IndieAuthors
World

Dedicated to my family and friends.

Can anyone predict how the butterfly effect impacts families?

Can a family outrun its genes?

Like the phoenix from the ashes, we shall rise again.

Prologue

The house was so quiet you could hear a pin drop. Arianna dozed with one eye open, as only new mothers can. She stirred with an exasperated sigh when she heard the initial murmuring, then quiet as a mouse, moved across the cool floor with great stealth. The autumn chill made her shiver, then wrap her arms tightly around herself.

Passing strangers could have observed Arianna's shadow against the lilac painted wall, creeping from her room to his – a witch-like image – her hair tied on top of her head, resembling a hat. Halloween was just around the corner. Remaining hopeful of getting back to sleep, she stayed quiet. *Please make him settle*, she prayed. She'd never been so tired.

She crept towards the beautiful white cot, tastefully decorated with contrasting pale-blue quilt and bumper. Arianna pressed the button on the mobile and the lullaby hummed softly in the background, along with brightly coloured images projected onto the matching walls. The night light shone like a beacon from the corner of the room. Looking down, the young mum noticed her baby was no longer still, quickly retrieved the blue dummy and popped it in his mouth. Heading towards the door ready to leave the room, she stepped on a squeaky floorboard, stopped, held her breath and stood very still, until the baby's breathing was back to the rhythmic sound of suck, pause, suck, pause. Imagining his chubby wee cheeks going in and out, Arianna continued to wait for another few minutes. Satisfied he'd settled, she moved towards the door hoping for a sharp exit – instead the door squeaked in the stillness of night. The whimpering from the baby meant repeating the process once more. Another chance at a quick exit.

This was not to be the case.

She admitted defeat and brought him into her bed, lay back down cuddling them both together as one, confident the closeness of being with his mum and the warmth of their bodies would soon put him back to sleep. It did, until an involuntary movement from her arm stirred the little bundle. The dummy was spat out and replaced with a curled-up tongue and a wide-mouthed yell.

Before she placed the loud-mouthed monster back in his cot, Arianna said, 'Stop crying, stop it. Please stop.' She paced with him, repeating the words over and over until she had no strength left. Desperate, she put him back in the cot, where he only wailed louder.

'Stop!' she screamed sitting back in her own bed next door with her pillow in front of her.

The decibels only climbed higher.

She stomped into the room. 'Be quiet! What do you want? Go to sleep, you have been fed.'

Leaving the baby's room, she screamed in desperation, 'SHUT UP!'

Louder and louder they both cried. Arianna reached for a tissue, angrily wiping the tears away, but the aloe vera scent had no impact in soothing the situation.

Going back into the room to the red-faced monster lying in the cot, who'd kicked off the covers, evoked feelings of hatred towards Toby who just wouldn't stop.

Frantic, pacing back and forwards, now back in her own room, Arianna rushed around grabbing clothes and hurriedly dressing, before going down the stairs.

'Shut up, Toby. Will you just shut up! Why did they make me keep you? I can't deal with this!'

She ran up and down the stairs, then opened the front door, ready to run. The cool air hit her with a jolt. She closed the door and ran back up the stairs, the screaming still coming from the cot. Picking him up, he momentarily stopped and gasped.

Then the crying started all over again.

'What do you want?' she screamed, winding the mobile up, but the soft lullaby did nothing at that point to defuse the distress in the room.

'Just stop.

'PLEASE!'

Her bag packed, she glanced at him in his cot. *What am I going to do?* she thought in desperation. She turned and walked away. At the bottom of the stairs, she angrily ran her hands through her hair, then rubbed her face in anguish.

Toby, exhausted from crying, stopped and the house returned to complete silence.

'If only you'd stopped earlier we would have been fine!' she wailed. 'Why didn't you just shut up? I needed you to stop. Mum and Dad should be back soon; they know what to do.'

Going into the room to retrieve the money being saved for a camera, about to descend the stairs, Arianna was suddenly aware of the humming sound of the mobile along with the bright shapes swirling on the ceiling. Toby was captivated, stretching his hands out towards her.

'I never asked for you, Toby.'

The baby reached out again and started simpering.

'I DON'T WANT YOU!' Arianna screamed in desperation. 'I want Mum and Dad.'

She paced up and down the room saying, 'I never wanted you,' over and over again.

Finally, decision made, she grabbed his snowsuit from the wardrobe and stuffed him in it. Toby started to murmur in protest.

'Lie still and shut up.'

Once he was zipped, she propped him against her shoulder, headed back downstairs, grabbed a bottle of formula and left the house.

Waiting at the empty bus stop, she stamped her feet to try to get some warmth in her toes.

A bus eventually approached, windows steamy, nearly full, with jovial chatter from people ready for Saturday night fun, like her parents.

A sequinned high-heeled figure, walking past her seat, cooed at Toby. 'Aw isn't he cute!'

'Look at him all cosy,' said another passenger with a smile.

Arianna turned and looked as loud singing from football fans at the back of the bus disturbed the peace, their warring anthems jarring.

'What you looking at?' one of them yelled down the bus. 'Oy! I said what you looking at?'

'Leave the lassie alone, Dug, her wean's asleep.'

Finally, after an uncomfortable journey, they arrived at the final destination: the hospital at the top of the hill.

Ready to get home, the driver shouted, 'Everyone off!' He opened his cab, stood up and stretched with a loud sigh.

'We're going, pal!' The singing got louder and louder as they moved forwards.

Inebriated Dug said, 'Sorry, hen,' as he passed.

The driver nodded at the sleeping baby. 'All quiet on the western front. Come on, lass, you need to get off, I'm finished for the night.'

Arianna nodded and warily left the bus, uncertain about what she was doing. With nowhere to go, silent tears welled up and spilled onto the baby while walking round the town.

'Could we go to the hospital?' she asked the sleeping bundle, his heaviness dragging her down.

The NHS neon lights shone 'Welcome'. Decision made, destination reached and uphill struggle over, Arianna stopped to sit by the entrance, hoping people-watching would help calm her nerves. It was hopeless as the swishing of the doors and cold draught started to irritate her. Unaware of her distress, the porter, in his pale-green and navy trousers, briskly en route somewhere, nodded at her. 'Evening, how are you?'

'Hmm, good, thanks.'

Arianna got up and started to wander aimlessly, thankful for open visiting hours for dying patients so she didn't look out of place.

Two nurses, deep in conversation, passed her by, oblivious. Doctors in white coats with stethoscopes sticking out of their pockets turned right towards the sign saying 'Theatre'.

Another porter dropped the metal lid of a bucket, the sound startling Arianna. 'Sorry, darling, hope that didn't wake the wee one.' Arianna shook her head.

She noticed the toilets. Entering and using the cubicle was difficult with a baby and he began to stir. Placing him on the floor, she opened the door. The taps came on full force and sprayed water everywhere.

'Damn,' she said rather louder than intended.

Instinctively knowing they were alone, she tiptoed back towards the baby, lifted him into the cubicle and closed the door just in time, as she heard someone enter to use the facilities.

She waited nervously to hear the door close, while placing the clothes and food beside Toby.

Leaving her problems behind in the cubicle, Arianna moved towards the swishing of the door and into the cooler air.

She found the overnight bus waiting with the engine quietly purring.

'Single, please.' Arianna boarded the bus with less weight on her shoulders. Ticket in hand, she sat down with a loud sigh and braced herself for the long journey ahead.

Chapter One

Every Saturday night the girls met outside the local disco.

Susan entered the disco, her friend giggling as she trailed behind her. The girl behind the counter greeted them, 'Oh, hi, Susan, are you putting your jacket in?'

'Yes please.' She handed over a fifty pence piece and received her raffle ticket. A line of jackets hung on metal coat hangers. Matching raffle tickets strategically placed over the crook, assuring the correct jacket would be returned to its rightful owner.

The flashing lights and glitterball struck the girls as they opened the doors and saw lines of dancers mimicking the actions of 'Night Fever' by the Bee Gees. Maybe John Travolta would be inside.

'Wow!'

The girls shouted in unison, 'Come on. Let's go!'

Bags on the floor, safely in front, the girls jumped on the spot to the sound of the next song: 'Off the Wall' by Michael Jackson.

'I love this!' Susan shouted over the noise.

'What?'

'I love this one!' Susan screamed.

The dance floor was heaving, the crowd clearly enjoying the beat, hips swinging, hands up, moving from side to side, the music pumped through their bodies. Everyone there for another great night. Susan scanned the crowd, observing familiar, and some new, faces.

Empty glasses meant it was Susan's round. 'What do you want to drink?'

'Same again,' hollered her friend.

Approaching the bar, crowds three deep were hard to dodge. Susan stepped over the sticky gooey mess. Jason, observing the most stunning girl he had ever seen, was amused as he watched her dodge the mob.

Susan smiled across at the handsome man watching her from the opposite side of the bar. Her smile was quickly reciprocated with a grin and a wink.

The barman eventually asked, 'What can I get you?'

Susan pointed and shouted above the loud din, 'Two more, please.' The barman got the gist from the actions required on such busy nights.

Juggling the drinks, the change from five pounds, and then stepping on the sticky floor, Susan found the glass slipped out of her hand onto the counter.

Jason appeared beside her and signalled to the barman to help. Mopping up the spill with an already wet cloth only smeared the sticky liquid around the bar.

Before the barman disappeared, Jason secured a second drink and handed it over.

'Thanks,' replied Susan.

'You're welcome. The last dance is mine, is that a deal?' The handsome stranger smiled. They both simultaneously felt the tingle, like a jolt of electricity, as they passed over the drinks.

'Deal, see you later.' She smiled.

Finding a seat, the girls finished their drinks before resuming the Pan's People dance routines. The adrenalin pumped through their veins in time to the music, which made both girls feel so alive. Quick glances towards the bar confirmed she was in fact being watched, which caused embarrassment.

The DJ announced last orders at the bar, then, 'Last dance. Grab your partners for "Still" by the Commodores.'

Jason walked towards Susan as promised, asking for the last dance.

She was overwhelmed, about to dance so close to this gorgeous guy. Her heart was pounding, her mouth dry. When asked she merely nodded, then followed him onto the dance floor. His pal asked the other girl to dance.

Dancing over, they finished off their drinks, then went to get their jackets. Queuing was no pleasure with sore feet.

'Ticket please,' asked the girl behind the counter.

A girl at the front of the crowd pleaded, 'I've lost my ticket. It's that one over there.' She pointed.

'You'll need to wait until everyone with tickets is served,' replied the cloakroom attendant.

Huffing and puffing, the girl replied, 'You have got to be joking.'

'No,' the girl behind the counter said. 'Made that mistake once, person hot-footed it with a luxury jacket, believe me that was no joke.'

'Move out the way, we have a taxi to catch,' said Jason.

'Cheeky get! So do I.' The girl's eyes rolled in disgust. 'I paid my fifty pence the same as you, pal.'

Waving the ticket above his head, Jason said, 'You should have kept this safer, pal.'

Susan was next to get her jacket before the four of them made their way to the taxi rank.

'Great night, girls, don't you think?' Jason's friend asked.

'Amazing,' Susan's pal replied, swaying and being propped up by last dance boy.

Once in the warm vehicle, the taxi ride proved very interesting.

'What time do you finish tonight, driver?' asked last dance boy.

'Around three o'clock once the taxi rank clears,' replied the chipper man.

'This is the girl I'm going to marry,' Jason exclaimed. Susan giggled and snuggled into him.

'Been going out long?'

'We met tonight,' Jason replied.

'Met the wife forty years ago and we said the same.'

'REALLY?' asked a surprised Susan.

'I wasn't always this age.' The taxi driver laughed.

Susan blushed. 'Sorry, I hope that wasn't cheeky.'

'Not at all, believe me the years pass before you know.'

'No offence, driver. What age are you?' Jason boldly asked, the drink making him appear cocky.

'Turned sixty last month.'

'Sixty!' Jason laughed.

'Listen, son, I was once your age, thought anyone over thirty was old!'

'Just drop us here, driver. We'll walk the rest of the way.' Pushing the fare between the seats, he said, 'Keep the change.'

'Thanks. See you again,' said the now amused driver.

It felt so easy. They walked and chatted by the light of the moon, exchanging a kiss and telephone numbers before they parted.

The next day, Jason phoned and they chatted about all sorts for an hour.

Interrupting her swooning around singing 'Still' by the Commodores, Susan's mum asked, 'How was your night, Susan?'

'Mum, it was amazing. Jason told the taxi driver we are going to get married.' She giggled and repeated a lot of what Jason had talked about on the phone. This handsome guy was going to marry her.

Ah loves young dream, her mum thought fondly.

The pattern of the evening calls quickly became routine over the next week. On Wednesday night, after nearly two hours, Dad popped his head out into the hallway and pointed to his pretend watch, signalling that it was bedtime as everyone had work the following morning. Susan took another ten minutes to finish the conversation. Her voice fluttered with excitement, overheard by her parents in the kitchen, tidying away supper dishes before bed.

The following Saturday, the preening and constant changing of clothes suggested a second date was on the cards. Jason duly arrived at seven.

Her mum opened the door, proffering her hand. 'It's a pleasure to meet you, you must be Jason.'

'Yip, that's me,' came the cocky reply.

'In you come,' she said to Jason, leading him down the hallway and into the living room.

'Susan!' she called. 'Jason is here, love.'

'Thanks, just be a minute.'

'Hello, lad, take a seat.' Dad jumped up with gusto, a bit nervous to be meeting the illustrious young man who'd been on the other end of the telephone line all week with his daughter.

'Pleased to meet you, sir,' said a less cocky Jason.

They all sat watching the television in the corner, when an advert for Milkybar chocolate came on.

'Do you like that chocolate?' Jason asked nervously. 'I love white chocolate. That boy is so cool, waving his lasso around.'

'Mm yeh we do,' replied both parents in unison.

Thankfully, at that moment, Susan appeared in the room, stunningly dressed for the occasion.

'Ready?' said Susan.

'Born ready,' replied Jason before they both left for the evening.

After they left, the parents looked at each other, unsure about what they had just observed.

Once outside, the young couple headed to the local pub. They walked and talked with ease, their conversations an extension from their telephone chatter. They both felt familiar and secure within a short space of time. Tonight they were en route to meet last dance boy and his now girlfriend for 'one' before going onto the disco. The girls hugged on arrival, and the boys nodded. This was to become a familiar routine over the coming months.

Arriving first and waiting for their friends the following week, the chat casually turned to travel.

'I fancy throwing the towel in and travelling round the world in my own little boat, bobbing up and down on the ocean.'

Giggling, Susan replied, 'Count me in, that would be so cool, Jason.'

'Really?' He sounded surprised.

'Definitely,' said the love-drunk young girl, cuddling in closer as they snuggled together on the seat. 'I have worked since I was sixteen, you get tired of the rat race, Jason.'

'Aw I don't feel like that, I stayed on at school before starting at the firm, so it still feels quite exciting.'

Susan looked over and noticed her friend scanning the crowd, then stood up and waved to catch their attention. Once their friends arrived the conversation moved on.

A few weeks later, Jason asked her to meet him at the pub.

The whiff of newly sprayed perfume arrived in the living room before Susan. Hoping for a quick getaway, she popped only her head round the door.

'Don't pop your head round, come on in,' chirped her dad. 'Susan, you can't go out so scantily clad, given you are just getting over the cold.' His stern tone sounded fake. 'Where are you going anyway?'

'Out to the disco.'

'Disco! That's not dancing. Your mum and I, we actually danced the night away.'

'Oh for heaven's sake, Dad, times have changed since you two rocked around the clock or was it rocked until ten o'clock?'

'Very funny.' Her mum beamed.

'Remember, you and I could have won any competition at Blackpool Tower Ballroom in our day,' says Dad, winking at mum. Both mum and daughter have a strong resemblance to

Demi Moore. Mum smiles at her husband, while remembering the good old days.

'"Footloose and fancy free," your gran used to say, Susan.'

Mum's thoughts turned away from the current pretend argument to wonder, do times really change, or do the same things happen from generation to generation? Her own dad opened the door and chased her husband away when he was her young man. He was firmly told there were chores or hair washing to be done. Sprinting to the bedroom window to see him, a regular game ensued of blowing pretend kisses to each other. They then smiled and waved goodbye. This was reciprocated with a bow, before he turned away. Knowing next week, they would link up at the local ballroom. After the dancing they walked home together week after week. This pattern was known as courting, before eventually marrying. It took years for her dad to like that young buck, who needed brought down a peg or two, with coiffed hair and a swagger on him like he owned the town.

'Mum …'

'Sorry, love, what is it?'

'Bye. See you later.'

She was guaranteed a quick exit as *The Morecombe & Wise Show* started soon. Both parents knew nothing stops young people dancing the night away.

'Susan, please put on that warm coat,' her mum pleaded.

'Mum, stop.'

Hearing his chortling, Susan asked, 'What's so funny, Dad?'

'Do you still get a supper these days? Remember, Mum? It was great. Pie and beans or peas included in the price of our ticket.'

'Those were the days, my friends, we thought they would never end,' Mary Hopkins sang from the television in the corner.

'Even Mary Hopkins agrees!' Her dad gave another hearty chuckle. 'How many times did Bobby have fifteen pints and a pie?' He looked across to his wife. 'Then the next day it was hard not to laugh when he claimed the pie was off when he was sick.'

Her mum and dad both start spluttering at the memory, saying in unison, 'That was so funny. He said it every week.' Both laughed again.

Susan moved to the other side of the door, shouting towards the living room, 'It is different, discos stay open till midnight.'

'Susan.'

'WHAT?' she said with an exasperated sigh. 'What is it this time, Dad?'

'Terrible. They should shut at a decent hour like in our day!'

'Things are different, stop barking on about the past. Even when I came back with this lovely cheesecloth top and jeans your standard answer that everything costs a fiver annoys me. It's much more expensive. This cost me £6.99 for the top alone. Don't say it, Dad, just don't, your jokes are so bad.'

Her dad chuckled and Susan feigned annoyance. When he chuckled again, she feigned annoyance before laughing.

Right on cue, he smiled cheekily and uttered the usual retort, 'Did you also get a free haircut with it?'

'Byee byee!'

Closing the door, the escapee caused a draught in the living room, which made the striped brown and cream curtains flutter. The house was fashionably furnished with smoked glass tables and a beautiful brown and beige suite, which toned in perfectly. The display cabinet doubled up as a drinks cabinet when they had the traditional New Year party for their friends old and new.

It was hard not to laugh before Susan made a getaway. Dad knew he would have done the same back then.

'Were we like that?' his wife asked.

'Of course,' he responds, 'probably worse.'

Nudging him playfully, she said, 'You were, I wasn't. You still look good, not too shabby for a Saturday night.'

The maturing years had been kind to both. He puffed out his chest, which made her laugh. The compliment had been well received, he still looked dapper. Clean shaven, smelling of Old Spice and wearing his favourite Levi jeans.

Chapter Two

All hospital wards in the 1980s were painted an insipid magnolia. Many badly needed touched up or completely repainted. Chipped paint or broken plaster flaked every time a freshly made bed bashed against it. Red brick effect, cold concrete floors were everywhere. Washed daily, then dried quickly to prevent infection. Fresh air entered via open cream-painted sash windows. All wards were set out in rows, beds one foot apart. Overhead, metal rails had curtains, which swished giving the illusion of privacy, regardless that all conversations were overheard.

The ward sister was immaculate, in her sparkling white uniform and frilly hat. Morag feared trouble seeing sister's reflection against the window, and instantly jumped up.

'Morag, no need to jump.'

'Sister, em okay,' said the young auxiliary nurse, a schoolgirl the month before. A petite girl with brown eyes, her hair cut into a bob.

'Morag, continue as you were,' said the observant sister to the young worker, in a rather authoritative tone. The tone belied her relaxed mannerisms, as sister's soft, white shoes gently glided along the corridor. Stopping to tenderly fix a plant on the windowsill, hanging to one side desperate for daylight. Morag was unnerved by the brusque tone, stirring feelings of unfamiliarity in this new working environment. The expectation was for independent learning, understanding different boundaries.

Sister, overhearing the conversation progress, turned back and smiled. Confident this new recruit oozed a natural flair. Morag smiling back, felt a wave of happiness, which boosted her confidence. With a sigh of relief, the young auxiliary nurse crouched back down beside Mary's chair. Taking the bony, callused hand of the patient, Morag's soft tender hand touched and soothed the distressed patient almost instantly.

'Did you know, lass, I was a nurse?' the elderly lady asked.

'I did. Remember you told me TB patients in the sanatorium had their beds pushed outside overnight when they were convalescing.'

'Did I tell you that, lass? The young ones now, you know,' she whispered, 'they don't have a clue.'

'You did share that with me, but some of us do have a clue,' replied the smiling, quietly spoken girl.

'You are right, lass. I was like you.'

Continuing to chat to Mary meant she lost all sense of time. Colleagues, now standing with black and red capes slung round their shoulders, waited patiently. First break would be over if Morag didn't hurry. Together they made their way to the refectory and selected dinner. The pungent smell today was of overcooked cabbage and braised links. Not a favourite, so the majority chose pie, beans and chips. They all sat at the maple-coloured veneer table with matching chairs, strategically placed with enough space for staff on staggered breaks. All exhausted after a hard shift, the conversation at points became a venting session.

'This is my tenth day on,' said Sandra.

'I was so tired last week, here, there and everywhere, no staff as usual, I couldn't even go dancing,' said Kim.

'Watch this space, I'm going out in about two hours,' said Margaret.

Staff morale was high, which brought immense pleasure most days. The radio's piped music was heard throughout the hospital. Staff hummed softly along to the tunes, while making the beds. Lifelong friendships were secured as they sorted laundry and dusted, and further kindled and secured on work nights out.

'Don't forget to put in for an early next week for Marie's leaving do.'

'I completely forgot about that. Morag, can you swap a back for an early shift,' said Sandra.

'Sure,' said Morag.

'That's great. Will you put it in the off duty book so sister can change it?'

'Will do it as soon as we get back to the ward.'

'Please, don't forget,' begged her friend. 'Thanks, Morag, you're a pal. Have you gone for the long stand yet?'

'Yes, last week,' said the youngster. 'It wasn't until I saw Kim and Margaret laughing ... I knew then it was a trick,' Morag said.

'No, you didn't,' Kim and Margaret teased.

'Oh you two leave her alone,' interjected the jovial tones from the other two at the table.

Morag blushed.

The rest of the evening passed without many requests for bed pans. With half an hour to go before the end of her shift, Margaret disappeared into the toilet. She washed and changed, then emerged from the bathroom. The citrusy, floral scent arrived before the suitably fashionable disco queen.

'You smell good. What's that?' asked Kim.

'My new perfume, Yardley Tramp.'

As the smell wafted around, Margaret moved up and down, watching the clock until it was time. Quick as a flash she was gone.

***

Some months later, life was simple for Morag. She had a good job and contributed to the household overheads, waiting patiently to meet a lad, get married and have children. Morag was part of a close family, who went to worship every Sunday and lived by the values promoted by the church.

They fitted in well within the community and never dreamed of doing anything out of the ordinary. Dad worked full-time. Mum worked part-time to supplement Dad's wage. The weekly menu started with mince on a Monday and finished with a roast on a Sunday. This routine never changed, that would be deemed too daring and financially irresponsible by her parents. Every Saturday they got 'spruced up', before taking a short walk to the bowling club in time for the second act.

On her now regular weekly night out, Morag saw him before he saw her. Her heart thumped in her chest to the beat of the music. Her brain silently screamed, *Is that 'my' Chris? Oh my goodness, what is he doing here? All those days spent following you around like a love sick puppy, and you're here.* Embarrassment took over as the heat travelled from her head to her toes. Her flushed complexion was nothing to do with the heat of the disco, but the fact he was approaching.

She quickly turned to face the poster on the wall, pretending to read about upcoming events and hoped he would pass. But a tap on the shoulder made her turn and there in front of her stood 'her' Chris.

'I know you! Did I see you at the hospital? I work there too,' said the young lad.

'Oh, oh, hi, it's you!' Morag replied with a startled look.

'Yes, it's me,' said Chris, lowering his eyes and looking himself up and down, as if to confirm his presence.

Bashful and blushing, Morag hoped Chris never found out about her crush on him.

'Ah, I remember now why you looked familiar. Did you not used to follow me round the corridor when we were at school?'

'Mm,' Morag replied, mortified while pretending to be unsure what he meant.

'Hi, I'm Chris.'

'Morag. Pleased to meet you. I need to get back.'

Having now been formally introduced, they walked back in single file before disappearing in different directions to join their friends.

On Monday, it was as if the universe lined up. They literally ran into each other when Morag was on her way to the laundry to search for missing clothes. Chris and Morag chatted, lingering in the corridor, comparing notes of the band from the previous Saturday. Both agreed the band were amazing. Next time, they would go together. About to say goodbye, both enquired where the other was going. It turned out the same place. Chris said he was en route to check an electrical fault in the laundry room. They walked along side by side, an easiness growing between them. Over the next few weeks, their paths crossed more frequently, in fact almost every day. With no reasonable explanation, Morag was becoming increasingly convinced it was serendipity. The day Chris appeared in the ward, staff noticed a change in the new start's behaviour. So endearing was this, that some of the married staff suggested they ask him if he was single. Morag blushed and fumbled so much, it confirmed their suspicions, a true love story in the making. Saffron made the cunning and nefarious plan. Initially asking Chris's number for a friend who was looking for an electrician to help with a new washing machine. The innocent young man parted with the digits to the house phone. Next Saffron asked Morag for her number for a friend who was looking for someone to babysit and thought she might be able to help on her days off. Morag, unsure how she would manage this, given the shift work, willingly gave her phone number, not wanting to disappoint her new friend.

The following night the phone rang just after teatime.

'Hullo, you looking for an electrician? I was given your number, em, do you need, em, help with a washing machine?'

'No, who is this?' said the young girl.

'It's Chris. I was given your number by Saffron from work.'

'Chris, its Morag.'

'Oh doh,' he said. 'I can't believe that Saffron.'

'Saffron! Let me get the number she gave me. Is this your number? I was told to phone as you needed a babysitter.'

They chatted for ages on the phone. *Ah*, thought Morag, *a romance made in heaven like in Jackie magazine.* What started as a crush on a schoolboy, was about to turn into the story of her dreams. The anticipation, wondering where and when they would next meet was exhilarating. Round the corner, the canteen, or walking home from work. Today he waved and called from the other side of the street.

'Oh hi, Morag, how are you today?'

'Good thanks, you?'

'I'm good, thanks.'

They walked together before going their separate ways. Both lingered as if there was something hanging in the air between them, unsure what it was, until Chris finally plucked up the courage to ask her out.

'Fancy going to the movies on Saturday?' With bated breath, he waited for the rejection to come.

'I would like that, Chris.'

The sigh of relief made her realise he was nervous.

They started going out regularly. A weekly trip to the pictures was her preferred choice. They ambled along. The only thing was the kiss she had dreamt of, instead of taking her breath away, felt more like being kissed by a slobbery dog. Practice makes perfect 'Jackie' told her. They just needed to keep going. A small hiccup, she was sure could be overcome.

'How is the courting going, Morag?' said mum.

'Mum.'

'Why don't you bring your young man home on Sunday for dinner?'

Morag would pretend to think about the suggestion, however had no intentions as going out with Chris provided such delight. To be seen around town was far more important. They went to the pictures, for walks and ice cream. Sensing a restlessness, Chris seemed less enchanted.

'Fancy going in for a pint and a gin and tonic?'

'No, I'm okay thanks.'

'Really?'

'Yes, really Chris.'

They continued to date. Nevertheless, there was no real spark between them. It felt more like a contented friendship. Given her family dynamics, Morag thought this was as good as it gets. Feeling guilty, she agreed to bring Chris home for tea and biscuits. This satisfied the parents and kept her dreams alive.

Chatting one evening, Chris said, 'Do you remember Dave?'

'No, don't know him,' said Morag.

'He joined the team a couple of weeks ago.'

'Can't place him, Chris.'

'He's a really cool guy,' Chris confirmed.

At home, Dave tried desperately hard to look like his idol, Clint Eastwood, imitating his mannerisms, the walk, his hair combed in a similar style. Once preened and hair sorted, his sister would laugh at him. Trying almost bashfully to fit in through school meant being on the periphery. Neither part of the in-crowd nor unable to project a confidence. This un-assured young man became a loner. It was difficult, going between classes, as some of the other boys would be a bit rough and would think it was funny. *The sooner I leave this place the better,* consumed his every thought.

As a result, one night when the family were round the table having dinner his mum asked, 'Why the sad face, son?'

'I'm leaving school when I'm sixteen,' said Dave.

'Only if you have a job,' his dad replied.

'I know, you have already said that, Dad.'

'You know the score, no loafing about here all day, lying in bed. A job or back to school, that's the rule.'

Determined to succeed, Dave found work, leaving school at sixteen. His first job was a Youth Training Scheme (YTS) programme. In a factory bringing in just £10.00 more than dole money, paid as unemployment benefit. Frustrated others in the place were earning a decent wage, meant Dave was delighted by a chance meeting in town.

'Hi, Chris. How are things?'

'Great. Got work at the hospital after I left school. You?' said Chris.

'That's great, mate. Any jobs going?'

'You looking for something else?' said Chris.

'Hate my job and no money in it.'

'Give me your number,' said Chris.

The next day Chris made enquires, resulting in securing permanent employment in the hospital for Dave. They went to the local pub. The bar had pool tables and a few melamine tables, basic and uninviting. He told Morag about the plans to meet Dave, inviting her along. They all played pool, losing a game each. Dave was near Morag who was trying unsuccessfully to pot the blue ball. 'I can't reach,' she said, looking at Chris.

'Here, let me help you,' said Dave, unaware she was gazing at his strong physique. He then showed her how to hold the cue, and, when their hands touched, both felt an electrical pulse pass between them. Nothing to do with the polyester clothes they were both wearing.

It felt good having a pint with Dave. They laughed and joked, then at the end of the night, he also paid as a thank you to Chris for his help.

When they finally parted, the young guy said, 'Cheers, mate,' shook Chris's hand and nodded towards his girlfriend standing by his side who just smiled.

'See you Monday, Chris, you're a good mate.'

'You would do the same for me.'

'For sure.'

Chris then turned. 'I had a great night, Morag, and you are quite good at pool.'

'Cheeky!' she said, then took his arm as they walked home.

Dave's mantra of work hard, play hard, meant spending all his money between Thursday and Sunday, then borrowing every week from his parents till pay day. Now having secured this new job, with a significant pay rise, meant he had enough to survive most weeks without borrowing from his parents. A double delight, discovering Morag also worked in another area of the hospital. Their first encounter was on the Wednesday. They passed in the corridor with a friendly exchange, a day he never forgot.

'Morag.'

'Dave.'

'What a great night I had with you two, plus you are not too shabby at pool!'

Morag giggled with embarrassment. Once they said their goodbyes and parted, Dave lingered and watched Morag. A happy self-assured girl. Blissfully unaware of the magnetism she exuded, making her even more attractive to him.

The three of them went out a couple of times to play pool, sometimes for a drink. Sharing stories of life in the hospital and all the antics, Morag told them about the long stand. 'You never fell for that,' they both said as if the lads were now highly experienced workers. Dave didn't mention that he had been sent for a set of left-handed pliers. Morag and Chris changed their weekly routine, going to the pictures every Friday, then dancing on a Saturday if her shifts allowed. One particular meeting stuck out to both Dave and Morag, a fond memory they would later retell with Dave acting the fool and bowing like a jester.

'Hi, Dave, how are you today?'

'All the better for seeing you.'

'Aw thanks, Dave, you've made my day.'

With a bow, he said, 'My pleasure.'

A beaming smile from both suggested feelings were emerging. They did nothing about it. Morag continued to go out with Chris. Feelings of guilt were beginning to consume her as she would never deliberately hurt her boyfriend.

'I saw Dave at work today. He agreed that was another great night. We must do it again soon, eh?'

'Yeh, he said that to me too,' replied Chris.

'Are we going to meet him again soon, Chris?'

'Maybe.'

Morag was still not brave enough to break up with Chris, therefore continued as they had always done. Chris had some feelings for Morag, but treated her like a mate rather than the love of his life and never felt jealous. They kissed, which had improved but wasn't fulfilling. They cuddled; he was like a loveable teddy bear. Morag believed in keeping intimacy for that traditional special night, the wedding night. Retrospectively this may have been a sign of how close they were as friends.

Meanwhile, Dave and Morag seemed to be searching each other out more at work. The beaming smile every time they met made both hearts jump with pleasure. This mutual admiration continued along with flushes of emotion every day, as the quick chats lingered on. Morag realised she really liked Chris as a friend. Their relationship was no more than a superficial romantic notion. No strong connections or emotions towards each other. This then allowed Morag to pluck up the courage the next Saturday.

'Chris, I think we should finish.'

'Finish what?'

'This,' she said, pointing from herself towards him.

Clearly not listening, distracted by looking at the paper to find the latest movie to go and see, he replied, 'If you want.'

'If I want; what do you want?'

'Same as you.'

'CHRIS!'

He jumped.

Looking around the room at the unmade bed, the yellow candlewick cover trailed on the floor. Cups and plates, piles of books, magazines in the corner made her look closely at him for the first time. The one thing intact was above his head, attached to the wall with drawing pins, pictures of his hero.

'Great, isn't he?' he said after he noticed her looking at the pictures.

'Who?' she said, irritated.

'Clint Eastwood.'

Morag then looked at his current choice of clothing. Levi jeans and cap-sleeved white tea shirt, it was clear he was trying to replicate his idol.

'Do you think I look like him?'

'Yeh, I suppose.'

'Cheers.'

'Do you still want to go to the pictures then matey?' He laughed.

'No, Chris, I don't think we should.'

They never did, but they continued to chat at work. It was over as quickly as it started, with neither feeling any real sadness. *Strange,* thought Morag, *when you hanker after someone, to find it isn't always what you imagined.* Their friendship petered out when Chris began dating someone else. They eventually married and moved away. Occasionally, Morag met them on return visits. Once the initial, *Hi, how are you? What are you up to?* conversations were over, they really had nothing much to say, apart from Chris saying, 'Tell Dave I am asking for him.' Dave, on the other hand, was completely different from Chris in every way, carrying a dream he would one day marry Morag.

At work two weeks later, they met.

'How is Chris?' said Dave.

'We finished a couple of weeks ago,' said Morag.

'He never said.'

Morag in a rush had to leave it at that and said her goodbyes, but the following day, they met again. This time Dave said, 'Would you like to go to the pictures with me?'

'I would, Dave. When?'

'What about Saturday? The Clint Eastwood movie is getting good reviews.'

'Okay, what time?'

'Get you at 7.00 at the Towns house.'

'That's a date.'

The weather was warm and sunny and they strolled along side by side, chatting about all sorts.

'Do you like working at the hospital?' said Dave.

'I do. What about you?'

'If I'm honest the work is just okay, but I like the money,' he said.

Walking so close together appeared to trigger static electrical impulses which passed between them. Arriving at the box office, the poster promoted the movie 'Every Which Way but Loose'.

This had a picture of an orangutan with one arm around Clint Eastwood, leaning affectionately towards him.

Their selected seats were at the back. Morag stumbled, dropping some of her popcorn, it was hard to see, going from the daylight to the darkness of the picture house.

On the way home the chatter began again.

'Did you enjoy the movie?' he said.

'Yes, I liked it, particularly when the orangutan heard the words "Right turn, Clyde."' She laughed.

'I liked the bit with the old granny,' he said.

'That was funny!'

He walked her to the bus stop. They had a quick kiss before they parted, with him going in the opposite direction. Once on the bus, she gazed out the window, they smiled and waved. He waited for her bus to depart before leaving.

Going home on the bus she thought about Dave. Was he also trying to be Clint Eastwood by wearing Levi jeans and a white t-shirt?

She arrived home in a good mood.

'Did you have a good night, love?' her mum asked.

'It was great,' said Morag, hanging her coat on the stand before going into the kitchen and opening the fridge.

Mum came in and sat back down to finish her supper. Morag noticed her mum was finding comfort in touching the yellow melamine table. They had saved hard to buy the matching chairs. Mum was distracted, running her hand up and down the table admiring the new purchase. Smooth and sleek it added glamour and comfort to the kitchen. The black speck provided a lovely contrast. Morag moved the bottle of camp coffee, to expose the dimpled glass sugar bowl and cream jug both full as she reached over.

'Watch, Morag, that doesn't spill.'

'Sorry, Mum,' said Morag.

'Sit down and tell me about your night,' said mum enthusiastically.

Morag lifted two digestive biscuits, but they slipped onto the table and smashed. Gathering up the pieces, she sat across from her mum.

'The movie was funny. I laughed all the way through.'

'I hope not too loudly or the audience would have missed the next joke.'

'MUM!' she said in mock frustration.

'Aw, love, you know I'm joking, your loud belly laugh keeps me amused. How was Chris?'

'MUM! We broke up two weeks ago.'

'Oh, that's right. It was Dan you were going out with tonight, wasn't it?'

'Dave.'

'Oh, this is not going well, Morag, is it?' Her mum chuckled.

'No, Mum, it's not.' Morag reached over and took her mum's hand. A soft tender hand met another soft tender hand. One wrinkled, the other smooth. The love passed between them. Morag got up and kissed and cuddled her mum before saying goodnight.

Then the daily calls from Dave began. Sometimes she called him.

'Were you trying to look like Clint Eastwood on Saturday?' She giggled.

'A bit. I look like him, don't I?' came Dave's sullen reply.

'Not really!' She chuckled again.

The silence unnerved her.

'I think I do,' said the dejected voice down the line.

'Perhaps just a little bit,' Morag said, cheering him up temporarily.

After another fifteen minutes Dave said he would need to go. 'Byeee,' he said, lingering on the phone.

Morag was next with her long goodbye. 'You hang up first,' she said.

'No, you hang up first.'

'Let's do it together, after three …'

With that they were both gone for the night. These conversations solidified their relationship over the coming months. Both were smitten and besotted, assuring each other they would never get old. They would always watch *Top of the Pops*. The day they stopped would suggest they were getting old.

Very quickly, the sparks between them were electrifying, both falling very much in love. The kisses and cuddles were a complete contrast to Chris. In going out with Dave a respectable two weeks after breaking up with Chris, would she discover agreeing so quickly could have regrettable consequences?

They came together to visit soon after. Mum was keen to meet her new beau. Feeling unusually nervous, her mum did her best when entering the living room. The hostess trolley was set. A plate of sandwiches, plain and chocolate biscuits underneath with a full teapot on top. They chatted and her mum started to relax.

'Would you like a sandwich or a custard cream, Chris?'

'Mum, its Dave,' said her embarrassed daughter.

'Of course, Dan, help yourself.'

'Dave, Dosy, Beeky, Mick and Tich,' Dad oddly chipped in.

'DAD,' said Morag, completely mortified. *I will never do this to my children,* she thought.

'Do you like The Monkees, Dave?'

Before he could reply, her dad said, 'Please help yourself to another custard cream, son. Welcome to the family.'

Mum looked over with slightly watery eyes. Dad smiled and nodded. His wife reciprocated, acknowledging he had again managed to pull them out of an awkward situation with a bit of humour.

Chapter Three

J ason picked Susan up from work in his shiny new car. Looking out the office window at five to five, Susan waved before putting the document into the manila file and safely locking it in the tall grey metal filing cabinet, in date order and alphabetically listed. It was exactly five o'clock when she exited the building.

Opening the new car door, slight apprehension took over as the smell from the red leather seats slightly overpowered. The shiny metallic green was pristine. Maybe he could call it a Christmas name, given the combinations of colours. To be discussed later. Before saying a silent prayer, *Please God, don't let me catch my high heel on the new paint.* This meant she lifted her legs in an exaggerated way over the tread, falling into the seat. He laughed at her antics.

'Hi, Jason. Wow, this is smashing!' She sighed, exhausted with trying to get into the car.

'Do you really like it?' Slightly unsure how to react, Jason puffed out his chest. This new purchase was getting the desperately needed seal of approval. He was extremely happy.

'Love it,' she uttered.

The purring from the new engine was mesmerising to the young couple. They eventually chatted about their upcoming nuptials. The wedding was to be a relatively quiet affair. Keen that his parents be in attendance, the young bride again enquired about changing the date to accommodate Jason's mum and dad – to a time when they weren't on their annual holiday to the caravan. Susan thought this strange, given her parents were to have pride of place at the top table.

'Why not wait?'

'No. They can change their plans if they want to come, Susan.'

Jason dropped her home. Susan leaned over and they shared a kiss. He would pick her up again at seven to go for a drive.

Entering through the back door into the kitchen, the aroma of the familiar cooking smells made her hungry.

'Oh, Mum, that smells great.'

Her mum smiled. 'Before you go upstairs, can we have a word, my darling girl?'

Susan sensed their unhappiness.

'We hoped when your big day came it would be extra special, but it feels very rushed, Susan.'

Mum and dad had been talking and weren't impressed with Jason. Getting married without waiting till his parents could be in attendance saddened them. Their latest fashion statement was where dad was sitting doing the crossword. The new melamine kitchen table. He looked up and smiled before interjecting.

'I can see beyond those pearly whites, he will break your heart one day, mark my words.'

'Dad, enough, it took Grandpa a long time to like you. Surely that would make you give Jason a chance,' their daughter pleaded.

'Mm, you're my girl. I won't allow that lad to hurt you, Susan.'

'Dad, he won't. He is so amazing,' Susan said, dreamy eyed.

They accepted Susan's enthusiasm. After tea all three went back over the extensive list, many of the plans already underway. Registry office was booked. Cake ordered. Flowers from a local florist ordered. A four-star local hotel on the outskirts of town for after the ceremony would double up providing opportunities for memorable photographs, to last a lifetime. The honeymoon also paid for was in another five-star hotel abroad. Susan would get the best send off. Mum and Dad had been saving for this special day all her life – the policy had recently matured, providing a tidy sum with very little to add from the savings account.

The toot from the car at seven o'clock on the dot meant the wedding plans were averted and popped into the folder. The conversation would continue the next evening.

Grabbing her coat, Susan quickly kissed both parents. Then the love-struck teenager disappeared.

'Oh hi, Jason.' She giggled, getting into the car more elegantly this time.

He nodded and smiled with the music blaring. 'Bat Out of Hell' was playing on the car radio and with that they were gone. The windows down, both enjoyed the feeling of freedom the breeze gave. They drove to the beach. The silence now meant they chatted about the progress of their wedding plans.

Jason then said, enthusiasm rising in his voice, 'Susan, listen, don't you love the sound of the waves lapping? Fancy a pirate's life for us? Over the seas and faraway?'

'Mm, yeh, that would be nice,' she replied, sounding less excited. Changing the subject, she asked, 'Do you want a red carnation for the buttonhole? It will match my flowers and Mum's outfit.'

'If you want. I'm easy.'

'Okay, another thing sorted, the florist intimated we will get a discount buying them all in that colour, so that's great, Jason.'

The wedding day arrived at great speed. Exhilaration from the young couple was tangible to all in attendance. This wonderful partnership would last a lifetime. His parents never attended.

Mum first in, turned and looked behind her to soak up the ambience and every moment. Starting with the moment her beloved daughter made her grand entrance. As they walked down the aisle, Susan held onto her dad, and the illuminated room was magical. Strings of fairy lights glistened and glowed. Both the bride and groom completed the image, making the room look stunning. The whole day from start to finish turned out to be a fabulous event. The bride and groom's photograph was in the local paper two weeks later.

***

On her return to work, in the coffee break Violet flicked through the local paper. 'You certainly looked stunning, Susan.'

'Aw thanks,' she said, leaning over to see the photograph of her. Both smiled like Cheshire Cats. 'I've brought my album in if you want to see the photographs at lunchtime?'

'Oh yes,' replied all the staff looking dreamy eyed.

'Your photograph in the paper is beautiful. Can't wait to see the album,' said Violet. 'They were very quick getting them back to you.'

'I know,' said the new bride, taking the album carefully out of the Grafton's carrier bag to show the office staff during lunchtime.

'Make sure your paws are clean before you touch,' said Jasmine.

'Shut up, we know without you trying to stick your oar in,' said Violet.

Even though Violet objected, she knew her friend Jasmine was right. Each person gently touched the paper that separated the photographs to reveal one perfect image after another.

'Tell us all about it,' they all said in unison.

Susan started by saying, 'It was very traditional. I arrived in the black wedding car. Dad threw the scramble of coppers for the children as we drove away.'

'Aw, that's lovely,' they all said at the same time. Then laughed at their precision. After all, it was an office used to the accuracy of facts and figures.

'It gets better. More romantic, girls,' said the young bride. 'Dad said in the car he was about to deliver his treasure to her Prince Charming.'

'Aw, that's so romantic. Your wee dad looks proud as punch,' said Lorna, swooning.

'Look at your eyes, Susan, shining like diamonds. Jason is also really handsome with that suit, the frilled shirt and red bow tie,' Violet said, with such warmth and affection. All the girls in the office loved weddings. 'Aw, that white lace dress fitted you to perfection. It certainly accentuates your petite figure.'

'Ooh accentuates!' Jasmine playfully mocked.

'It does.' Violet blushed, then added, 'Just saying.'

'I know, I'm joking, don't be so touchy,' said Jasmine before turning the page. 'What a vision, absolutely stunning, look at that skull cap and the floating veil. I know that wasn't by default, Susan, the bouquet of red and white flowers complemented both your mum and Jason's colours. Look, girls, closely at that cut and flair on her mum's outfit.'

An indication no expense was spared in the celebration of her only daughter's big day.

Lunchtime over, Susan carefully replaced the album in the box, then into the Grafton's bag ready for the return journey home.

***

Returning from their honeymoon, Susan and Jason invited her parents for Sunday dinner in their newly furnished house, which had a very nautical feel, both in décor and the ornaments around the room.

'It has to be quench blue and surfin' throughout,' Jason told the builder. The clock on the mantelpiece was of a ship's wheel. The picture frame holding the smiling couple was outlined in white and blue.

'What do you think, Mum?' Susan enthused.

'It's stunning, and what a spectacular view of the coast from this hilltop, beautiful like you, my darling girl.' Affectionately she held her girl's hand, then squeezed it gently.

'I second that,' said her dad as he approached and kissed Susan on the top of her head. His new son-in-law also approached and pulled Susan close, subtly moving away from the in-laws. Susan oozed with enthusiasm about their brand-new house as they waved her parents off.

'Look at this, Susan.' Jason pointed to the view.

'I know,' she said, cuddling into her new husband. 'We are so lucky, Jason, it's stunning.'

On the journey home, her parents chatted over their reservations again, but they also recognised they had successfully made Jason feel welcome as part of their family. Susan never questioned them. At times both parents remained quiet. They never said much about Jason, instead they listened to Susan and agreed at the appropriate times. One particular Sunday at their house, both individually left the room on the pretence of going to the toilet as they were livid listening to the buffoon.

A year later their daughter excitedly broke the news about being pregnant.

Jason tried to sound jokey, but it fell flat and there was an embarrassing silence after he said, 'Susan, you know me, I just wanted it to be us. Where you can continue to spoil me, pipe, slippers, dinner on the table. Off on our travels at every opportunity. We have enough money and could travel the world, going over the seven seas and far away on our adventures of a lifetime.' He winked.

Sensing her parents were not amused, she too started to pretend. Susan smiled and played along. 'Baby makes three, over the sea and far away.'

The dessert Susan had spent a while preparing did not sweeten the situation. Mum and Dad saw through her feigned smile. They were concerned for their daughter. Yet, observed such love for Jason and hoped he would grow up when the baby arrived. When leaving that day, Susan kissed them both at the door saying, 'Don't worry, we'll be okay.'

'We hope so, darling.'

'Byee, see you soon.'

'Bye,' shouted Jason from the living room.

Chapter Four

The pregnancy progressed with the only difficulty getting comfortable in bed at night. Things changed, with less talk of adventures after finding out she was pregnant. Jason's reaction was not always as the expectant mum expected. This frightened Susan, however she felt sure when baby arrived it would settle.

'I want to guarantee I will always be around, Susan.'

'What do you mean, Jason?'

'You know I didn't want a family just now.'

'Please, Jason, stop, you're scaring me.'

'Why?'

'Would you leave me?'

'No.'

'Aw that's good,' she said with a big sigh of relief.

The more the pregnancy progressed this sadly, was being said on more than one occasion. Particularly when she rolled into his back and the baby kicked him. She laughed but he scowled. She apologised, he accepted, and they kissed and went to sleep.

'Susan, this was not the plan. It was just to be me and you forever,' he whined.

***

They were sitting one evening watching TV and eating their usual snacks. The labour started two weeks after the due date. Only Jason and Susan were allowed into the labour suite. Her mum and dad were very restless. It was also said at the antenatal classes that it is a dangerous journey for baby. They empathised, having had their own stillborn babies.

The call came through from Jason. Baby made his appearance at 9.05 p.m. The next day, they met baby Oliver for the first time. Susan looked exhausted. Sitting in the ward with all the other mothers and babies, the photographer asked to take a picture of the mum, dad and baby for the local paper. This new family of three sat amongst other shots the following week in the paper.

'Can we lift him, darling?' asked the excited gran after kissing her daughter on the cheek.

'Yes.' Susan got up, lifted the tightly swaddled baby. 'Meet your gran.'

'Oh, look at him!'

'Come on, my turn.' Taking the baby, her dad said, 'A wee treasure from a wee treasure.'

'Meet your grandpa, Oliver. You'd best get used to his awful jokes!'

'Leave the lad alone. He and I will be great pals, you wait and see.'

About fifteen minutes before visiting finished, the new grandparents, both clearly besotted, gathered their belongings and said, 'We will get on and let you two have time with the wee laddie.'

Rest and bonding time for mother and baby were doctor's orders, before they came home to make a family of three. Readjustments were necessary, from being a couple to a family. The arguments started when Oliver disturbed the whole house as a new baby. Jason became quieter at home once Oliver was born.

'You okay, Jason?'

'Mm, just watching this. I'll be up in a minute.'

Hours passed and at the one o'clock feed frustrated Susan placed Oliver on Jason's lap, then went back to bed, saying, 'Your turn. I'm exhausted.'

'Bring his bottle then.' Which she did.

***

Over the next few months, being at home with baby, the change was gradual. Susan couldn't understand what was unnerving her, while Jason was always restless.

'What is it, Jason?' she would ask when they were lying in bed.

'Nothing, just thinking.'

'You are happy, aren't you?'

'You know I am.'

'I keep feeling there is something wrong with you.'

'He annoys me,' he said, pointing to Oliver's room.

'He's a baby, Jason.'

'Are you hankering after the travelling again, Susan?' Jason dropped in when they saw a boat in the clouds. 'You did say baby makes three and we could go.'

'Jason, that was before Oliver came along. He is content, we all are, aren't we?'

'Mm,' said Jason. The young couple had always been sensible. They had no money worries and had saved a tidy wee sum in the bank. Jason occasionally lamented about hating the rat race and would love to live off the land. Then he talked about giving up work and travelling, and Susan went along with the pretence of the assigned role; Mrs Crusoe. It was, she believed, after all, a private joke between them.

'Once Oliver is older, he will love going on the boat, Jason.'

'Aye aye, shiver me timbers!' He laughed before they dissolved into laughter.

***

It happened. A day she would never forget. The house felt eerily quiet after returning from the shops, provisions in hand. Oliver slept in the pram outside in the garden. Entering, instinctively she knew something wasn't right. The sparse wardrobe confirmed Jason wasn't home. The letter on the bed said he needed a bit of time away, that he was bored. He promised he would return.

Grabbing for the phone, hysterical crying quickly took over. 'MUM MUM MUM, GONE!'

Panic overtook as she thought her grandson had been abducted.

'Who, love? Shh shh shh, breathe, Susan. Who's gone?' Mum enquired, listening to sobs so painful to hear.

'JASON!'

There served no purpose hearing them condemn the father of this wonderful little boy. Her heartbroken parents watched Susan become a very good mother to Oliver. A drastic turn for the worst ensued; an empty bank account and the man gone. Susan was heartbroken, felt foolish and ashamed. The family never really spoke about that day again. The much-loved baby Oliver brought a wonderful dimension to all their lives. Work no longer a luxury, instead, became a necessity to keep the roof over their heads. The young mum worked very hard to provide a very comfortable life for them both. When Oliver asked about his dad she used to sing to him, 'When I was one I had some fun before I went to sea, I climbed aboard a pirate ship, and the captain said to me. This way, that way, backwards and forwards, over the rolling sea, a bottle of rum to fill my tum, and that's the life for me'. Both giggled and laughed as she did all the actions.

***

With the passing years, Oliver never really asked much about dad, accepting it was him and mum. He could be overheard, in the living room, telling friends his dad was a pirate. This meant popularity with the pals who loved to hear stories about him.

Oliver grew up thinking his dad was a pirate, he went to sea, drank some rum and never came back. That's how he remembered it. As the years passed, he was never really that bothered to ask what happened. Always thought it might upset his mum. He had a faint memory of many postcards from the Caribbean being in the toy box that he wouldn't let his mum discard. Said they were from pirate Jason who was going to come back and get him one day on his ship. They would go and fight sharks.

The first postcard when it arrived, simply stated:

'Bought a boat and sailed off into the sunset. You would love this life, Susan and Oliver, my precious cargo. Love J.'

She stowed it away, never telling her parents who already thought he was a fool.

At first they arrived regularly. Then they became less frequent. Until unexpectedly, one day when Susan arrived home from work, a postcard of a tropical island was lying on the mat behind the front door. Feelings of hope rose, along with impending doom. To steady her sea legs, she sat on the stairs. Staring at the beautiful photograph, the tears began to slowly seep from the corner of her eyes. The memories came flooding back, to the point Susan could actually feel the warmth of the sun on her back. Imagined drinking and tasting the pina coladas and getting caught in the rain. Memories of them as they giggled and laughed, Jason loved their recklessness. They had that life. Susan felt the warm salty tears run down her cheeks. She turned it over, hoping it would read '*Coming home. Missed you both, love Jason*'.

The dawning realisation hit. Her parents who never judged were right. She flipped the picture of paradise over to read:

> '*No homecoming party necessary, won't be coming back, have found my soul mate in paradise. If you want a divorce, Susan, you will have to pay for it as I'm skint and living off the land – The coconuts are amazing and the fish from the sea are scrummy. I feel like a right old Robinson Crusoe.*'

***

At the time, a devastated Susan took some time off work to recover. No hot chicken soup could heal this pain. The first Monday back, the young mum collected her son from her parents' home. Entering through the back door, Susan smiled hearing her mum and dad engage with the baby. They all sounded happy in the living room. Susan popped her head through the hatch, which joined the kitchen and living room. She quickly washed her hands, then placed the plated dinner into the microwave before entering the other room, where her mum had just fed the baby.

'Well hello, Oliver,' his Gran cooed.

'Come on, pass him over, diddly di de dum,' hummed Grandpa, jiggling the baby from side to side.

The young mum fretted as she entered, 'Dad, stop, he's just been fed.'

'Oh, Susan, don't be so serious.'

A burp, followed by sick projected onto grandpa's jumper.

'Told you!' Mum and daughter both laughed.

Susan ate while her mum changed baby Oliver into fresh clothes.

Susan kissed them both. Saying thank you, tinged with sadness.

'Aw, love, no need to thank us,' said her tearful mum, 'we will never know how hard it's been for you.'

Dad cleared his throat of any emotion, then stepped forward, kissing the top of her head while he cuddled this wonderful young mum.

'I couldn't have done it without you both.

'It was hard going back to work.'

'We know that, love, but you did it,' said Dad.

Chapter Five

Morag and Dave welcomed their new baby, Anne, along with twin boys Mark and Michael within five years. Morag and Dave created a happy little family. Anne toddled, then ran every night to meet Dave on his arrival home.

Coming home filled this dad with such happiness, along with the wonderful smell of homemade dinners, which were on the hob or about to be started. Depending on the kind of day Morag had had with the children. Being a mother was the best job she could ever have. Her children filled her heart with love and pride as they reached each milestone. It was hard work and sometimes she had very difficult days. On such days, Morag was glad when bedtime came for her children.

Dave's arrival home soon became a familiar routine.

'Is this the welcoming committee?' he said.

'It sure is, love,' said Morag, as she gave him a kiss before he scooped Anne into his arms.

'How's my little popsicle today? Effervescent as ever?'

'Me good.'

'I'm good,' dad would say.

'You good too,' replied the wee one.

The hallway was in a constant state of flux, due to limited space and a growing family. Clothes were on the treads ready to go upstairs. The pram held two contented, sleeping babies. Morag spent a lot of time trying to reorganise it to no avail.

The standing joke emerged. With deep affection Dave would say Anne was the love of his life ... 'After your mum of course.'

'Better be after me,' Morag said, playing along.

Entering the lounge, Dave sat on the chair and Anne jumped onto him. They both laughed heartily. Morag looked on lovingly, noticing their strong genetic resemblance – mid-brown hair and piercing blue eyes that shone like diamonds when they laughed.

As they cuddled close together, Morag squashed in beside them, and Anne playfully kicked her away.

'He is my husband, Anne.'

'No, my daddy,' said the wee one.

Mum scooped her up, then kissed her chubby wee cheeks. 'Come on, let's go and make dinner and you can help, would you like that?'

'I don't want vebbitles.'

Anne toddled over to her mum who caught her and cuddled her close, saying, 'Are you a rogue?'

Anne looked at her mum, smiled and nodded in agreement.

The phone then rang, Morag chatted to her mum before handing the phone to Anne. 'Can you come to my house and I will kiss your cheek?' she asked Nana. Morag assured her wee girl that tomorrow Nana would visit.

'Bring cake?' she asked her mum.

'Yes,' Nana said, 'tell the little darling I will bring Madeira cake over tomorrow.'

***

Over the years, Anne's friendship group solidified, having met in school. They started going to each other's houses when they were very young. Now at the age where their high-pitched laughter could be heard coming from the room.

'Keep it down, girls, you will wake the boys,' Morag would chide if it was getting too loud when round at Anne's house.

'Sorry, Mum,' she'd call before the high-pitched laughter continued.

Dave would get annoyed while Morag would say, 'Are they not better here, singing Spice Girls and Britney songs than running the streets with God knows who?'

'It does my head in, all this noise. They should all be in bed by nine.'

'Nine o'clock, Dave? They are teenagers,' she'd say before returning to her current Mills & Boon book.

At weekends the house was quieter as the girls met at the café. Anne was noisier coming home after the sugar rush. In the café loud chatter was heard as the music quickly energised the young crowd. The café owners never complained as the chi-ching of the till meant business was good. Oliver and the girls walked home. He could never understand the high-pitched laughter from the girls, who all at different points linked arms with him and jostled with him for being so serious.

'Oliver, smile,' said Hazel, 'your face won't crack!'

'Mm, I am happy.'

'Tell your face!' Caroline laughed.

This week the way they walked home Anne and Oliver were last. Arms linked all the way.

'Bye, Oliver. See you on Monday.'

'Bye, Anne,' he replied, then continued to walk home.

Anne liked Oliver, had done for some time, so was delighted to have walked with him arm in arm. Something stirred in her. She felt happier for some reason after they parted.

The change was subtle when they regularly became the last two. They chatted about music and school until it was time to part.

'Hi, love, did you have a good night? said her mum, coming down to make sure the door was locked.

'Yes. Oliver was saying Oasis are a great band.'

'Who's noasis?' said her tired mum.

'No, Mum, Oasis,' replied the love-struck teenager to her mum who followed her upstairs.

The following week, as Anne was getting ready to leave, the twins said, 'Oh, kiss kiss kiss. Oliver and Anne up a tree K I S S I N G!'

'MUM! What have you said?'

'Nothing,' an embarrassed Morag replied, realising the boys must have heard her tell Dave she thought Anne was falling for Oliver.

Before Anne left school, things took a turn in a very different direction from how it was planned her life would go. Her friends were great. Visiting regularly, they laughed and giggled like in their earlier school days. Their taste in music never changed. They became three instead of four, but that's another story.

Chapter Six

O ver the years, when Susan worked, Oliver spent a lot of time with Gran and Grandpa. Yearly, on Oliver's birthday, they enjoyed looking over the progress of the memory book. The plan was to present it to him on his twenty-first birthday. Sitting close together on the settee, they soaked in the memories while drinking tea and dunking chocolate digestive biscuits.

'Oh look, I remember his wee legs swinging that day,' said Gran. She smiled, delighted to have now built such a trove of wonderful memories.

The diary was getting bigger like their grandson. The enjoyment they both felt as they reminisced was cherished by them both.

'Do you think he will like it?'

'Oh look, he is about two there.' Grandpa smiled.

'When he was making a pretend cup of tea he toddled up to Susan and said, "Hi babes".' Grandpa laughed.

'Oh look at those wee cheeks, I wanted to eat him up,' replied Gran.

'I know.' Grandpa smiled, playfully nudging his wife.

Looking up from the photograph was a wee boy who started singing Happy Birthday and Grandpa said, 'It's not your birthday. It was last month and you were two'. Grandpa then said, 'Remember, he looked up with his big eyes and started singing, "Happy birthday, ga ga bears.".'

'Oh I've been sitting too long,' said Gran, then got up and stretched, having enjoyed the lost hours pouring over the memories of their 'little scamp'.

'I had forgotten about that,' said Grandpa as he touched the postcard. They'd bought it years ago, it depicted families in each of the windows of the tenement building. 'I did say when he was born we would be great pals.'

'You certainly did,' said his wife, leaning over to kiss him. 'I think you may have given him his love for buildings and future aspirations, love!'

'I think we've been blessed, he's a good laddie.'

'He is,' his wife replied affectionately, getting up and putting the memory book away for another year.

***

Grandpa and Oliver walked and talked over the years. They often stopped and discussed old buildings. Many hours were lost in the library, looking at the fabrication of buildings. Many interesting facts were covered by both on their many walks. With oodles of notes taken once home.

'Grandpa, it's so cold, yet if you hold your hand on it long enough, it warms up almost as if the building is alive.'

'It does indeed, lad, much like the people inside, don't you think?'

'For sure.'

'What would you like to work at, Oliver, when you're older?'

'An architect,' said the now inspired young boy.

***

One night not long after Jason left, Oliver was asleep and there was nothing worth watching on the television. Susan reminisced back to when things appeared perfect. Sheer frustration overwhelmed her as she shouted, 'WHY DID YOU LEAVE US, JASON? WHY?

'I hate you, Jason!' she screamed, looking round at all the nautical reminders. She threw the clock then instantly regretted breaking it, secretly hoping one day he would return.

Lying on the couch sobbing, a honeymoon conversation came to mind. Over drinks on the balcony as they waited for the sun to go down on another wonderful day, Jason shared how sad life had been for him. The cocky young man who irritated her parents was in fact a very insecure person.

'Susan, how lucky you are. Lots of love and happy vibes between you all.'

'Aw, Jason, I know they are great. It wasn't always easy. They did have stillborn babies.'

'My dad was horrible, always downed my mum. Mum would always say *let it be*.' Susan listened as he ranted and raved. 'I grew up in a family where my dad's dictatorial ways caused a constant undercurrent at home.'

'Why do you think that was?' asked the mystified young bride.

'He was forced to marry his pregnant girlfriend twenty-three years ago.'

'Ah, I see,' Susan replied, having done the sums – her husband would turn twenty-four soon.

'I made up my mind early on I was leaving as soon as I could. I will never be like him. I have worked hard and studied on the job to build up credibility along with qualifications. Susan, do you want to know how my leaving was received?'

'Tell me, Jason,' said the watery-eyed young girl who leaned over and rubbed her hand over his shoulder and down his arm.

'One less mouth to feed eh, Mother. Then the golden child, my sister, said, "Can I have his room?" Shocking as I wasn't even out the house, this was a week before I knew I had a place of my own. Dad was in bed and Mum spoke in a hushed voice, "I think I have found you a place to go, Jason". I was sixteen with no life experience. I joined the firm and moved up through the ranks. It was hard, Susan.'

'Well, put that all behind you, Jason. We're a team.'

'I know, Susan. We are sorted,' replied her young husband.

'I love being with you.'

'Ditto.'

Once back home Susan was still upset by Jason's story and felt a strong desire to visit his mum with the wedding photographs. They went in the new car, which purred along the road, and Susan could sense his nervousness. Before they reached their destination, his young bride took his hand and squeezed it.

Opening the door, Jason shouted, 'Hi, Mum, it's me.'

A bedraggled woman scurried out of the kitchen. 'Oh, hi, Jason. Hi, Susan, so very pleased to meet you again. Jason has told me all about your wonderful wedding. We were sorry to miss it.'

'Such a pity you couldn't come. We missed you,' said the bubbly young woman.

'Come on in.'

The atmosphere was tense. In the front room his mum had set a tray for afternoon tea. Home baking was also on the plate. Noticing the Grafton's carrier bag, Jason's mum quickly went and washed her hands, returned and rubbed them against her apron, to be doubly sure. Oozing with excitement, she gently opened the album which was placed on her lap. 'Oh look at those lights. What a magical photograph of you both, my handsome boy, and you are certainly a beautiful bride, Susan,' she said, lightly touching both their arms as she sat between them. Looking round the room, Susan observed the display cabinet; a Royal Doulton figurine collection while not her taste was admirable.

They ate, then waited a respectable time before saying, 'We need to get back to avoid the traffic.'

'Of course you do. Thanks for coming.

'Father, that's Jason and Susan going.'

'Cheerio.'

***

Once back in the car, Susan listened and felt very sad. He glanced at her with piercing jade green eyes full of sadness. This normal happy-go-lucky guy that Susan instantly fell in love with was wounded. Reaching over, she stroked his blond hair, then touched his bare arm to comfort him. His skin glowed with a summer tan.

After Jason left, Susan continued the contact with Oliver's grandma. An unspoken duty was felt one woman to another. It comprised of updating her mother-in-law of Oliver's progress. The cards arrived for birthdays and Christmas with money enclosed from his grandmother.

'Look, Mum, a card from Grandma.'

'That was kind, Oliver, you must remember to write and say thank you.'

'Yes, I will,' he replied, but sometimes as he got older Oliver had to be reminded.

Susan always sent school photographs, which she imagined would be put in the living room in the display cabinet beside the photographs of the other grandchildren. On the shelf above the Royal Doulton figurine collection.

Her mother-in-law assured her via their infrequent correspondence that was where the updated photograph was always placed. The reply was always similar – my oh my, Oliver is growing up so fast Susan. Please accept this wee something to help Oliver. Hope you are both well. Visit any time. A pleasantry which both knew would never happen.

The passing years came and went for Susan and Oliver. Oh, there were the usual ups and downs of the tantrums or the pals coming round to play. Even then, there was little noise as Oliver loved to play with Lego, building castles, pirate ships, houses and other things. He was a caring boy who never gave his mother any trouble.

***

Susan stayed with the same company, as did most of her now friends. Of late they'd begun to lament about how hard it was to discipline their children. She listened but stayed quiet at such times. Oliver was a textbook boy who never appeared to push the boundaries too much. Sometimes this was hard as they were her friends, and she did not want to gloat. This forced Susan to become skilled – with a nod to imply she understood, rather than risk another betrayal – like with Jason.

Her kind, loveable boy became her reason not to give up. They learned to work well together. For many years the established pattern was first home starts the evening meal.

'That smells great.'

'Mum, you made it. I just put it in the oven.'

'I know, darling. How was your day, son?'

'It was good. We looked at some European buildings, can you imagine what it must be like to see them, Mum?'

'Not really, Oliver, but I wouldn't mind visiting a shoe factory.'

'MUM, shoes!'

'BUILDINGS!' She laughed.

'If I become a successful architect, we can do lots.'

Later, doing the dishes, she handed back an unwashed plate.

'Mum, why are you doing that?'

'It's not clean.'

Frustrated, he took it and re-washed it as instructed. Susan rarely complained, knowing he was studying hard at school to pursue a career in architecture. However sometimes her patience was tested to the limit – his bedroom constantly littered with clothes and books. On some occasions she insisted that it must be cleared and his response never altered over the years.

'I will, Mum, you do know how busy I am studying.' Leaning over the top landing, he smiled, knowing it warmed his mum's heart. *He is some boy,* she thought, making her way back into the lounge to relax after a hard day.

***

The following Christmas, they got a surprise like no other.

Merry Christmas, Susan and Oliver, lots of love Gran and Grandpa, the envelope read.

'What is it?' both exclaimed.

'I bet it is tickets for the pantomime.'

'Oh not it's not!' Grandpa laughed.

The equally cheesy sense of humour meant the quick response from Oliver was appreciated by Grandpa, when he said, 'Oh yes it is!'

'MUM! DAD! That's far too expensive.'

'Susan, you need a break and we think you will love it.'

'Oh my goodness, thanks so much,' both said in unison when Susan handed the tickets of their first European holiday to Oliver.

'Means you can see some of those buildings you wax lyrical about, Oliver,' said Grandpa.

***

Travel soon became a passion for both. The hotel was beautiful. Once they unpacked the next morning, Oliver, who was normally a sensible boy, arrived at breakfast. Donning a hat with tassels strategically placed down both sides of his cheeks. Coming into the morning sun meant very quickly, sweat dripped slowly down onto the table.

'Oliver, take that off, you look ridiculous!'

'NO! I won't, Mum, stop. Everybody is looking at you. It looks cool.'

Susan particularly enjoyed the warm summer sun. Wearing this season's matching beachwear with panache.

They had such a wonderful holiday. Returning home, they both started saving for their next. Susan was so pleased, being able to secure an escape route from their day to day living, via package holiday deals over the next few years. These many welcome changes of location were wonderfully exhilarating.

It took them two days to relax into the holiday. The last bit of energy depleted from the daily toll of work and the now ever precarious balance of trying to secure a work/life balance. Away from a very busy world, which seemed to be getting busier by the year. Some, however, unfairly vented this at staff.

Oliver spent quite a bit of time in the room, while Susan, who loved people-watching, whiled away the time relaxing into the holiday. At breakfast, Susan tried to tempt Oliver with all the tasty food. 'This fruit tastes so sweet and juicy, Oliver. It's succulent and ripened to perfection by the sun. Do you want some?'

'No thanks, Mum.'

'Look at all the food up there.' Susan pointed at all the different stations. 'Over there, fruit and coffee, cooked over there and cereal over that side.'

'I will get something soon, Mum.' Which he did.

Without time constraints, people-watching would become a regular holiday pastime of Susan's. Exchanging smiles and pleasantries. That first holiday 'mishap' 4th July can still make them laugh.

***

Tonight is one such night. Reminiscing with some of the girls from work at Susan's for a girls' night and catch up away from the office. Drinks, chat and a bit of music. Susan was talking about their holidays when Oliver popped his head round.

'Hi, Aunties.'

'Oh, come here, give your old aunty a hug,' said Jasmine, jumping up. Oliver duly obliged. Then Violet jumped up. They had pulled out all the holiday albums.

Susan affectionately said to him, 'Go on, tell them again about the holiday mishap.'

'Are you ever going to let me forget that?' said the cheeky chap.

'That was so kind of your mum and dad. Bet they never knew they'd inadvertently funded two globetrotters.'

'Indeed,' agreed Jazz.

'It was so kind, Aunty Jazz. It gave Mum and me the holiday bug. Mm, I think they knew what they were doing, Mum, as they always gave me a holiday penny, which helped us a lot.'

'Aw, that truly was the case, Oliver, they did.'

Leaving the women to enjoy their night, Oliver went to his room. The chat downstairs was getting louder along with high-pitched laughter. Reaching up on top of the wardrobe, he lifted down his own memory book. The next few hours passed revelling with delight at the magical places they'd both visited.

> *Palma Majorica – 17th April*
> *The massive Santa Maria Cathedral was impressive as a Gothic landmark, which began in the 13th Century.*
> *Malta – 28th October*
> *Valetta in Malta and the wonderful outdoor auditorium, then the Royal theatre designed by English architect Edward Middleton Barry erected in 1866.*
> Oliver had noted in his book many facts and figures; including the fire that destroyed its original state.
> *Next year – Egypt Cairo 15th November*
> *Both mum and I were surprised. It was nothing like the brochures. An ancient place which appeared to belie the history attached to it. We were very disappointed,*

finding the pyramids on one side and a fast-food outlet across the road.

I was not keen on the area or the culture. Very male dominated. Mum was cautious. We never ventured out much and were glad to return home that year.

Oliver kept a scrapbook with notes, pictures and postcards of the buildings he saw on each trip. Which further reinforced his belief in pursuing a career in architecture.

The dreaded day came with natural progression. Oliver decided to go on his first holiday with friends. Susan mentioned at work that she was not going to go on holiday alone and some of the other women decided they would all go on a 'girls' holiday as Jazz and Violet had other family plans.

Susan was unsure, but Oliver's response was, 'I think you should go, Mum. Why not?' His reassurance and encouragement convinced her to go. She had a great time. The fun and nonsense meant they laughed till it hurt, so much so a similar pattern emerged over the coming years. A 'lightness' returned to her spirit – which Jason had stolen so many years before.

Regular holidays with several different groups of friends followed. The holiday clothes barely had time to dry before a quick turnaround.

Mum and Dad said, 'Susan, about time, you know we are always here for Oliver.'

'I know you are,' she replied with a smile at both of them.

On a couple of the holidays, Susan chatted to some different guys late into the night. One of them said, 'What a catch,' then apologised profusely due to nerves, saying, 'I am making you sound like a fish'. Both laughed heartily once the nervous tension passed. Phone numbers were exchanged to allow a meeting once home. On every occasion, after a couple of times, it soon became clear it was a holiday friendship that was never going to go anywhere. Sun, sea and sangria, then the dawning realisation that it clearly was not culturally transferable for Susan.

As Oliver continued through school, he talked more about going to university. The untidy room was frequently used as leverage. 'Oliver,' said Susan with a feigned stern tone, 'today, no excuses.'

'Mum,' her son smiled, turning his head sideways in a coy way, 'enjoy me while I am here because if I get into university, you will miss this mess.'

'I mean it, Oliver.'

Planning to complete the UCAS form in January, Oliver studied hard in his pursuit of architecture. From a very young age, he was fascinated by the construction of buildings. Diligently focused on the required grades in the exams. Passionately drawing rough drafts of his vision for future projects in his sketchbooks. Colour, texture, engineering, the light, glass and wood were all materials he loved to imagine working with. Susan worked hard to support this dream. He had been browsing through the sketchbook and holiday journals. Knowing his mum could not afford to fund him through university, made him begin to wonder if his aspirations could come to fruition. One evening after they finished their evening meal, Oliver must have been thinking again about the possibility of being able to go university.

'Do you think I may get a scholarship, Mum?' he asked.

'Maybe we will look into that. Oliver, we will make this happen. Even if we have to ask Gran and Grandpa for a loan.'

'No, Mum, I will get a Saturday job and start saving,' he said, which he dutifully did.

Susan thought at one time of becoming an accountant, having an insatiable love of working with figures. Meeting Jason and the path travelled put an end to that desire. In reality she ended up staying with one company and working up through promotions to become head of the accounts department.

'There's mail for you up there,' Oliver said, pointing to the mantelpiece. Susan opened it, then shrieked.

'Oh, Oliver, I have an interview next week for that job. Oh no, what if I don't get it?'

'Mum, stop worrying you are doing the job already, remember that. They need you, not the other way around.'

The naivety of youth made her laugh. 'Really, Oliver, will your Saturday job pay the mortgage?'

'Okay, you win 1-0 to you this time.' They both nudged each other and hugged.

After the interview, it took about a week to let the candidates know the outcome. Coming home, Susan saw the mail was lying on the mat.

'OLIVER! OLIVER!'

'What is it?' said the panicked teenager.

'COME QUICK!'

Dreading what he may find, Oliver started running down the stairs. 'MUM! You okay?'

'Da da,' said a triumphant Susan. 'You are now looking at the newly appointed—'

'MUM! I thought you were hurt,' said a now irritated Oliver.

'Oh, come on, let me have my moment of glory.'

'Not funny, Mum, don't do that again.'

Her career went from strength to strength. With each job promotion, Susan and Oliver afforded a few more luxuries. In the last few years, this slowly allowed for the expansion of her previously sparse wardrobe.

One night during tea after the first promotion, knowing they were both saving for Oliver to go to university, Susan felt guilty. She had seen an amazing pair of shoes in town and was tempted.

'What's wrong, Mum?'

'Nothing.'

'Come on, what is it?'

'I've seen a pair of expensive shoes.'

'Buy them.'

'Oh, I don't know if I should.'

'You got the promotion so treat yourself.'

'Thanks, son.'

Like a foolish teenager, she couldn't sleep, thinking about the potential gift to herself. Feeling extremely frivolous, something Susan was not used to, the next day she jumped into town at lunchtime. All afternoon she looked and smiled at the extravagant purchase under her desk, after buying her first pair of expensive shoes.

'ARE THEY?' exclaimed Jasmine.

Bashfully, the accounts manager replied, 'They are. I'm going to wear them tomorrow.'

The next day, Jasmine looked and looked again, saying, 'Look at those legs, Susan, why have you hidden them for so long?'

'Aw, thanks, Jasmine, that's kind. Do you like the shoes?'

'Love them. You wear them with such style and panache, my dear.'

The house was gradually transformed from the nautical haven to a more contemporary home over the years, given their limited budget for luxuries. Susan could not bring herself to accept financial support from her parents given their life savings had disappeared on the fairy-tale wedding, which never lasted.

Chapter Seven

At school, Oliver was always friendly with a group of girls, Hazel, Caroline, Anne and Dee. He 'went out' with Dee when they were in primary three.

Dee wrote, '*Will you go out with me?*' and the paper was then passed to Oliver, like a game of pass the parcel.

Oliver wrote one word at the bottom of the letter, '*Yes,*' then the note was hand-delivered back, like the music had started all over again, till the note reached its destination.

They were boyfriend and girlfriend until she 'chucked' him two weeks later for another boy in the class. He was upset at the time. This group of girls liked Oliver as a pal, which continued throughout primary school. Very early in secondary school, Dee and Oliver started going out again; a couple of times to the bowling, walking hand in hand, sharing a bashful kiss before parting. Oliver, awkward and shy, plucked up the courage to say he did not want to go out with her again. Dee did not like this and pleaded with Oliver to reconsider, to prevent being embarrassed that she had been 'chucked'.

'Oh no, Oliver, please can we go next week?'

'No, Dee, I don't want to.'

'I WILL. REMEMBER THIS. FOREVER!' she screamed before marching away.

A couple of years later, it naturally happened that Oliver and Anne ended up seated together every time they all met up at the local café.

It seemed overnight that the young man across town emerged. His voice broke and he started to broaden out. One Saturday, Susan and Oliver were in the car driving to a birthday party. On the return journey, Anne's name was yet again mentioned. Susan looked over lovingly at her boy, listening to the excitement in his voice, instinctively knowing her wee boy was growing up.

'Anne.'

'Yeees Anne.'

Anne's name came into the conversation every day after that. Anne this, Anne that and Anne the next thing. With eyes that shone every time he told a story with Anne in it. Along with weekly chance encounters in the supermarket with Anne and her parents during Saturday shopping trips. Coincidentally they began to meet every week just beyond the bread counter.

Oliver spoke first, then blushed.

The reply 'Hi' was always followed by a giggle from the young girl.

The parents nodded each week, then they all went their separate ways. Susan was aware of the start of this teenage romance.

'Hi, Susan.'

'Hi, Anne, how are you?'

'Good, thanks. You?'

'Good.'

Anne became a regular visitor. An easy person to get along with, Susan enjoyed the 'girl' chat about fashion, doubly delighted when Anne was keen to see Susan's shoe collection. Securing a friendship with Oliver's mum. Then there was the enjoyment of watching the two of them in the kitchen making supper where the usual early relationship bashfulness was endearing for Susan.

'Stop it, Oliver, I'm warning you,' said Anne.

'Oh stop it, ooooch, Annnne, do you think I'm scared?' said Oliver.

Silence was followed by laughter before sitting close together on the couch to eat their supper. They would nudge each other and laugh. Touch each other's arms, accidentally on purpose, then feign annoyance while smiling at each other.

'Mum, tell her.'

'Tell her what, Oliver, nothing to pick between the two of you, one is as bad as the other.'

'Muuum. That's not fair.'

'Ha ha, your mum's on my side.'

'Stop it, the both of you, before I bash your heads together in the hope it will knock some sense into you.'

Their relationship grew as they did. Until one day out of the blue Oliver told his mum that they were having a break, that studying needed to be his main focus.

'Mum, between work and study I don't have time.'

'How does Anne feel about this?'

'MUM!'

'What, Oliver?'

'Never mind,' said Oliver in frustration.

Intuitively knowing this was not the case, Susan noticed Oliver becoming quieter. The muffled sounds of crying at night when alone in his room confirmed something was wrong. This deeply sad situation affected them both. Trying to find an opportunity to speak as they did before was now met with an irritated young man's, 'Mum, I have to focus on getting into uni, I'm too young for that sort of thing.' Oliver then turned, quickly ran upstairs and closed his door with gusto and frustration.

Susan spoke to her parents to seek their advice.

Sighing, her mum reassured Susan. 'He's a good lad. It will be okay. Susan, you can't wrap him in cotton wool. Hard as it is to watch, Oliver will get hurt in life. It will make him stronger.'

'I know, but it's so hard to watch him looking so sad.'

'Mm,' said both parents in unison. 'We do know, darling.'

Over the next few months, their relationship was turbulent. Uncharacteristically, Oliver was up then down. Susan was beginning to worry that something wasn't right. Were her instincts right? What his mum didn't know, was that the telephone call the night before would certainly have confirmed her fears.

Chapter Eight

The one-way system in place was for security purposes. The pupils walked the corridors clockwise. The noise was deafening as the chatter of many conversations echoed in what little available space was left. There was also the scent of mixed fragrances, which didn't necessarily go together. People with allergies sneezed their way to class. The final smell was the stink of puberty. Anne deliberately stalled and missed the turnoff for class. Swept along in the crowd, Mondays now meant seeing Oliver twice before class. They began to smile in a different way, since their Saturday routine had become established. Mum dropped her at school, anytime she missed the bus.

'Come on, Anne, hurry we may still make it in time.'

'Okay,' mumbled the sleepy teenager.

'You need to be more organised and responsible, Anne. Do you hear me?'

Once in the car, the sullen, quiet teenager silently looked out the window.

'Oh, Anne, I loved this song,' crooned her mum, turning up the volume on the car cassette player.

'And they called it puppy love, just because we are in our teens,' sang Donny Osmond.

Trying to fill the gap of awkward silence, Mum prattled on. 'You know, Anne, Sunday routine, brush substituted as a microphone. While you imitated your favourite pop star as you looked in the mirror.'

Anne glared over at her mum. A wave of sadness came over her.

'Anne, I love you. What can I do to help? We will get through this I promise you.'

'WILL YOU STOP. JUST STOP ASKING, MUM!'

Everything had ticked along. Until Anne experienced turbulent, hormonal changes, which led to terrible teenage angst. In the house, her behaviour was torturous, a complete contrast to their previous, loveable little 'popsicle'.

'Where is my little popsicle?' said Dad.

'Go away, Dad.'

'Suit yourself. Get out to school or you will miss the bus, and if you do your mum will take you.'

'Dave, stop. I am not taking her again.'

Anne smiled slyly, deliberately missing the bus by walking slowly upstairs to collect her bag.

Lamenting to Cathy on the phone later that day, Morag said, 'She is constantly challenging my authority, its wearisome. Dave refuses to back me up in every unreasonable demand. It is hopeless, Cathy. This morning she deliberately missed the bus. Then smiled when Dave said I would take her.'

'Morag, it does get better.'

'When?'

'When they leave home,' said Cathy.

They both laughed, rant over, before moving onto the next topic for discussion.

What she never told Cathy was that Dave's final quip often was, 'If you don't like it, Morag, you know what you can do,' while pointing to the door.

***

One night, arriving home later than usual having been to Patsy's, her mother-in-law's, to drop off shopping – Anne was out, and the boys were in their rooms – Morag glanced round at the pristine kitchen and white goods. It was clear no one had even made an attempt to start tea. Morag was startled as Dave arrived, banging the front door shut. Clearly distressed, he questioned Morag who was putting away some shopping. 'Why are you just in?'

'Why are you asking?'

'I saw Chris and his wife in town. Have you seen him?'

'Oh not this again, Dave. Yes, I met them at the checkout in the supermarket. I was to pass on their regards. You haven't given me a minute to tell you.' Morag lost her temper. 'Stop it now, ranting and raving about the same issue from how many years ago. Too many to remember, yet you are still so bitter and resentful, grow up.'

The raised voices brought Michael down to enquire what was happening.

'Get lost, Mike.'

'Don't speak to him like that,' snarled Morag.

'I will and I can, so shut up, woman.'

Morag regained her composure. 'That's it, Dave, get your things and leave. I never want to see you again.'

He was dumbfounded. She had never spoken to him like that in front of any of their children. Michael said, 'Mum asked you to leave now go, Dad.'

Banging around like a petulant child, Dave packed a bag and booked a hotel in town. He raged, thinking this overnight stay would give Morag time to miss him and apologise. With that, he slammed the door shut and was gone. Dave walked away shocked, ashen and frightened. Once he calmed down, the first thought was Morag would have a lot of making up to do; the foolish woman. A bunch of Tesco finest flowers should do the trick on the return journey home tomorrow.

The next day did not go as planned. He opened the door, she looked at the flowers, took them from him and put them straight in the bin. Morag then reiterated, 'I meant what I said, Dave, it's over, has been for a long time. You have always been very difficult and constantly kept me down. I only put up with it because I didn't want my children to suffer.'

'You bitch!' he said. 'Are you running back to Chris?'

'Grow up, It's over. I don't even want to try again. I will only see you for the sake of the children.'

It took a while for her to move on after Dave left, in one sense there were feelings of relief; however, he had been the love of her life for so many years, yet sadly he never truly accepted that.

A pal let him stay 'sofa surfin'. Which held less appeal and wasn't as exciting as when they were younger. Dave tossed and turned, restless being out of his 'own' bed. Luckily the flat he then rented was furnished. Anger and rage consumed him. As a result, within a few weeks, he met a much younger woman. The adoration felt exhilarating. This wonderful new relationship excited him and quickly boosted the bruised ego. He believed the age difference was incidental.

'Stupid bitch, Morag, you don't know what you are missing.'

'Oh, Dave, this is a cool wee place,' said Tania on her first overnight. He didn't agree as he knew the bed was more comfortable back home.

Within a short period of time his new girlfriend moved in, becoming pregnant a few months later. Lying in bed, Tania's voice rose with excited baby talk each morning, which irked him. Panic set in, as it had been different with Morag. He encouraged his young lover to get rid of their unborn baby.

'NO WAY, DAVE!' she sobbed, then tearfully pined. 'My parents would go mental and hunt you down, Dave, we are such devout Christians.'

'Okay, okay, calm down,' said the impending father, the only reasonable choice left to take responsibility for his actions. Next, came feigned excitement with the extended family. Going along with numerous plans for this much loved and wanted baby. He had felt young again with the initial physical attraction, which had excited him. What an old fool he was.

'Dave, the pink or blue? Mm, maybe cream, we should stay neutral. What do you think?' said the excited, new-mum-to-be Tania from the other room. 'DAVE, can you come? I think we could get the cot in this way,' Tania said, pointing towards the window. 'What do you think, how many babies would you like? I think maybe two, or even three or four.'

Silence.

'Dave, are you listening? Don't forget to put in for leave of absence for the first scan.'

That night came profound sadness, loss of a previous life. Lying in bed as he faked sleep to deter the sexual advances of his much younger, vibrant partner, startled sleep followed. He was talking to Morag, the previous life had been retrieved and reconciled.

Waking with a start, his young lover was up on one elbow, saying, 'Dave, Dave, who were you talking to?'

In his dream Morag had welcomed him back home. They would have the new baby most weekends. This childish hanker even included thoughts of being so much kinder to Morag. After all they were good together, most of the time, except when he felt deeply insecure.

The thought of a new family was not nearly as satisfying. Unable to share this with the new partner, who was already talking about having at least three or four children, his life was turning out to be like one of Morag's favourite movies, *It's Complicated*. It certainly was, and he was no Alec Baldwin and she would never be his Meryl Streep again.

***

Anne was devastated when her dad left and blamed her mum. Another argument was about to erupt. All Morag had asked was that Anne take the clean washing on the stairs upstairs next time she was passing.

'You pushed Dad out after one argument. I will never forgive you.'

'Anne, you don't understand.'

'I do, you pushed him out, and now he's with Tania. You fooled us all. Dad was happy, it was you who wasn't.'

'That's not true, Anne.'

'I hate you both so much, you have ruined my life.'

'No, Anne, we haven't,' said a heartbroken mother, who was not about to disrespect her husband.

The teenager's emotions swung like a pendulum between sympathy, quickly changing to anger, then frustrated tears welled in her eyes. Promising herself this would never happen to any children she may have in the future.

The next day, having missed the school bus again, the atmosphere in the car was painfully quiet. Morag tried filling the gap to no avail.

'Drop me here, I can't listen to you anymore.'

'Bye, Anne,' said Morag, who burst into tears the minute the car door slammed closed.

After dropping Anne at school, Morag pulled the car into the side, crying uncontrollably, wondering did she really push Dave out?

***

The following weekend, Anne left the house that night in a cheerier mood.

'Bye, Mum, see you later.'

'Bye, Anne, hope you have fun.'

It was fun. Until much later into the night when Anne began to feel frightened and vulnerable. The streetlight outside the park was flickering. The amber glow was projecting shadows onto the ground and trees. The wind picked up, whistling through the trees. The rain started to go from a light drizzle to heavier rain. The sounds of the night were scary. Her breathing began to change as her heart beat faster and faster.

'Is there anyone there?' asked the frightened teenager. The group she was out with were not her regular pals. At the end of the night they had wanted her to leave with them.

'I'll catch you up, on you go.'

'Are you sure? Come on, let's help you up.'

'LEAVE. ME. ALONE!' shouted Anne.

'Leave her. Come on, let's go.'

I will get shelter under the tree till the storm passes, thought Anne. The ground underfoot was extremely muddy. Anne tried to sit down, slid sideways and ended up covered in mud. Trying to balance, she landed with a bump, which was sore. This triggered anger and sadness. Dad had left her. Now deeply distressed and muddy, tears sprung in her eyes, blurring her vision. Unsure if she had made it onto the ground, she put her hands down, now also covered in mud. Memories of happier days filled her heart with pain. They flickered through her mind so vividly, from before the babies were born. Cuddled up in Dad's chair; young Anne adored him. Having heard the story so many times meant it could be recalled instantly. Yet, tonight it brought no sense of consolation.

'DAD DAD DAD!' she wailed. Then decided to phone Oliver. 'Oliver, PLEASE, pick up my call and answer your phone,' she cried frantically. Dialling the same number over and over with no reply.

This teenager loved Oliver passionately. Consumed with rage that this late-night demand for help was being rebuked, irked her to the point that it didn't hurt that much when she started striking her arm against the tree. Irrationally thinking this would make him suffer for not coming to get her while loathing thoughts filled her head. They were finished. Oliver would learn the hard way. Many people would be willing to accompany her to parties and dances.

It didn't go as planned – the night became colder, then loneliness set in. No one came to carry her home. No support or familiarity, no reliable protector from the elements.

Eventually getting up onto her feet from under the tree, her resentment dissipated. While trying to assimilate her thoughts, Dad, Mum and Oliver. Completely confused, life had come to this. She wondered how it happened; how she ended up hating them all equally. Passing a door, someone called, 'Come into the party!' *Why not?* she thought, and going from there, went onto different house parties throughout the weekend.

Some arrogant individual at one of the houses laughed, while saying, 'What happened to you?'

'Fell in the park.'

'Aw that's okay,' mocked someone else. 'Thought maybe you had an accident.'

'Shut up, you can see it's mud,' replied the host. 'What's your poison? In there, help yourself, voddi or whatever.'

'Thanks.'

***

Arriving home, her mum insisted on taking Anne to the doctors, due to the bruising and swelling on her arm. She sulked, shouting, 'I am not going … you can't … make me.'

'OH! I CAN! LADY, GET, IN THE CAR, NOW!'

The stern look and bristling from her mum was futile, surrender quietly followed, going to the car without another word.

'Oh my goodness, what happened?' enquired the doctor.

'Hit it on a tree,' the sullen teenager replied.

The doctor prescribed strong painkillers and requested a trip to the local hospital to have Anne's arm X-rayed. The broken bone resulted in a visit to theatre that afternoon. Once home, she was allowed to stay in bed for the next few days.

Subsequently, two operations were required plus attending physiotherapy.

'If this had been treated right away, it would not have needed such drastic therapy,' said the consultant to the subdued teenager.

Avoiding eye contact with the doctor, Morag felt guilty, berating herself, knowing the separation from dad caused Anne to revolt. When walking back to the car, she asked, 'Anne, why didn't you call me?'

'Don't know,' whispered the broken spirited girl.

Once tucked up in bed, the maternal impulse to heal Anne's wounds resulted in chicken soup and warm lemonade at regular intervals.

'There you go, love,' said Morag before sitting on the bed. The teenager was unresponsive, which meant mum quickly left her alone. 'Don't forget to take your tablets, they will help.' Every four hours the prescribed medication was taken to heal the wounds.

This went on for some time. The drugs numbed Anne's pain, sending feelings of enjoyment once they were absorbed into her system. The youngster felt all 'woozy and warm'. Repeat prescriptions were given over an extensive period by various doctors who perceived the severity of the break could still be painful. A profound, lifelong understanding of the danger of this was to develop given what was still to come.

Going to school was becoming increasingly difficult. Full of hopeless feelings, of sadness permeating within her heart; different from when dad left. At the start of each new week, people laughed and mocked Anne, after hearing all about the weekend parties being frequented and the antics being participated in. Others gradually ignored her. Her friends from primary tried to help but were told to go away. They stopped asking.

'That's her, the girl with the 'brown' trousers,' they mocked and whispered when she passed.

'You should have seen the state of her on Friday night,' others said less quietly as she passed them in the corridors.

'Mum, my arm is sore I can't go,' she pleaded.

'Okay,' said Morag, who was now authorising more absences than attendances.

'I need to go home, my arm aches,' Anne said many times in the medical room.

When her mum was telephoned, she authorised the early release from school. As time passed, this change in behaviour was becoming the norm. Nevertheless, inwardly she became a lost soul, struggling to fit in while occasionally going to school. Parties with different acquaintances became the norm.

Morag called Dave and Tania answered. 'It's her, Dave,' she heard her deliberately say loudly.

'Hi, Dave, can you take Anne to stay with you for a bit? She is heartbroken and misses you,' said Morag.

'I'll get back to you.'

In the background she overheard, 'She better not be asking for Anne to come here, Dave.'

'Shsh.'

The reply that came, 'It wasn't convenient as they had a new baby and a puppy'. Morag was so annoyed at Dave, who happily went and picked Anne up from parties and dropped her off at home. Morag then had to listen to the constant, 'I wish I could just go and stay with Dad, he loves me more than you.' It took strength from Morag not to blurt out the truth. Obviously during this time the relationship between mother and daughter became very turbulent.

***

Morag made an appointment with the doctor and asked if they could do something as Anne had been on medication for such a long time. Morag feared a dependency had crept in. The records showed Anne had made appointments with several different doctors who had issued repeat prescriptions for over a year.

'I see what you mean,' said the sheepish doctor. 'I agree, your daughter does require to be weaned off them. It was a very traumatic injury, given the delay in seeking medical attention. This would have explained the extensive pain for quite some time after.' Dr Stevenson compassionately said, 'I will give you some leaflets for support groups in case your daughter suffers withdrawal symptoms.'

'Is that definitely going to happen, Doctor?' said Morag.

'Hard to say, depends on the individual,' said Dr Stevenson.

Morag tried leaving these around the house in places Anne would find them. Morag became extremely worried, finding the leaflets in the bin.

After that night in the park, Anne heard nothing from Oliver. They went their separate ways; the rejection meant Anne refused to conform to anything, by going to parties at weekends, consuming different types of alcohol in large quantities, along with the prescription medication. Nevertheless, Anne could not stop thinking about Oliver.

During the time they were apart, one night at the local disco, Oliver danced the last dance with Dee. She kissed him, hoping to go back out with him. Both were spotted by Hazel and Caroline.

Dee smugly passed the girls, en route to the toilet. 'What are you two gaping at?' she said.

'YOU,' said Caroline.

'Can I ask you, Dee, why Oliver?' said Hazel.

'All's fair in love and war,' she cackled.

The girls, disgusted, left without Dee, who was never part of the friendship group again.

***

A few weeks later at one of the many parties being frequented, Anne was in the kitchen to get a drink.

'Hi, Oliver,' said Anne.

'Hi, Anne,' he said, scanning the crowd, unsure what to say next.

'Sorry about calling you that night. I wanted to speak to you,' said Anne.

'Mmm, have things changed?' said Oliver.

'Ish, I am really trying, Oliver,' Anne said with an endearing softness to her voice.

The hours passed, and it still felt so easy being in his company, they talked and danced until the birds began to tweet their early morning greetings. Together, they saw the dawning of a new day.

'Have things changed?' he asked again.

'Ish, I told you.'

'Mm.'

This dashed any hopes for Anne that a romantic liaison was still possible. Oliver's words belied the sadness in his eyes that this had been nothing more than company at a party. They parted with Oliver saying he could no longer be her bolster. Being tempted by the easiness of being Oliver and Anne, he was glad it was April and the start of the Easter holidays and he wouldn't need to see her at school.

Foolishly, much later that day Anne returned to their usual spot and waited patiently full of hope. He never came and, after trying to phone Oliver to no avail, she was left deflated and angry. Once home alone in the cold bathroom, she looked in the mirror and caught a glimpse of someone she did not know anymore, even at fifteen going on sixteen.

Oliver couldn't stop thinking about Anne. He too had left earlier that day to go to their usual meeting spot, but got frightened, turned around and went home.

The spark was still there.

Easter came and went. The Monday routine was quickly re-established. Going round the corridors they smiled at each other. It re-ignited the embers within their hearts.

As a result, Anne went to Oliver's one day after the Easter break in April.

'Is your mum in?' said Anne.

'No working, why?' he said.

'I just wondered. Can I come in?' said Anne.

It didn't take long for the familiar feeling and strong sense of emotion to rise. They ended up not going back to school that afternoon.

'We shouldn't have done that,' Oliver said. 'Anne, we are over, till you sort yourself out and come off those painkillers.'

'I need them, they help my pain.'

'Really?' he said sardonically. 'Which pain? The arm or your dad leaving?'

'Shut up, Oliver, you don't know anything,' she raged as she looked at the displeasure on his face. She stormed out the room, down the stairs and slammed the door shut. Left alone in the room, his head bowed, the tears began to well, then fell from the scared, forlorn boy sitting on the bed.

Susan returned from work and instinctively knew Anne had been there. The lingering smell, the familiar scent, confirmed the youngsters' signature perfume.

'How's Anne? I do hope she is well. I haven't seen her for ages.'

'Dunno,' said Oliver.

'Was she here?' said Susan.

'Yes, to study this afternoon.'

Susan knew by the look on his face this was not the complete truth and decided not to probe.

Sensing his mum's unease he tried to sound nonchalant but unsuccessfully said, 'Busy studying for exams, think the break will be good for us, Mum.'

Susan knew it sounded contrived.

'Too young and all that, Mum,' he said with a sadness that sounded brighter and breezier than she knew he felt.

***

After their liaison, a rejected Anne was in school the next week studying level 5 play with a visiting lecturer from the local college. The woman asked the class to take out their teaching packs. Anne did not have hers, but refused the offer of a spare. Clearly not wanting to engage, Anne was then asked to move to another seat, but looking sullen, did not move. Repeating the instructions, the woman said, 'I gave you the choice, you refused the pack, now please move to another seat, Anne.'

She was repeating the instructions for a third time, as Mr Brannigan entered the room, looked around, got what he came for and left. Now the lecturer looked embarrassed. Anne still had not moved. The lecturer continued with the class. Returning two days later to teach another subject, she asked to speak to Anne outside the class.

'You know I promote a respectful learning environment, Anne? What happened on Tuesday? I offered you a spare pack, you did not want it. I asked you to move seats, you would not move. I can't have that behaviour, Anne. Mr Brannigan may now have the impression I cannot manage my class, which we both know isn't true. It was embarrassing, Anne.'

'I know, Miss, I am sorry,' said Anne.

'What happened?' said the woman.

'It's, just, Miss … em, em … I split up from my boyfriend because he won't put up with my shit – sorry. I love him so much. My dad and his girlfriend have a new baby, and they don't like me. My mum hates Dad. Doesn't say it, but I know. When he brings me home, I hate the way my mum looks at me with her big sad eyes. I hate my brothers. I am going to go and live with my gran if she will have me. I hate school.'

'Do you have a guidance tutor?'

'Yes.'

'You really should go and speak with them.'

'Thanks, Miss, I feel much better telling you that, it's like a weight's been lifted off my shoulders.'

Visibly sighing, Anne noticed tears glistening in the lecturer's eyes as she said, 'Okay let's go back into class.'

Anne, lighter in spirit, remained focused the rest of the afternoon and produced high quality work. It was evident she had a flair for Early Years. Informing the head of the school of the situation, the lecturer was reassured that speaking with Anne would be a priority. By the end of that week Anne sought help. The guidance tutor helped change her life by providing specific names of organisations who work collaboratively with young people in school. It proved really hard at times, due to Anne's poor communication skills. Being unable to articulate emotions, coupled with teenage hormonal disruption, made life difficult for Anne to comprehend while trying to change.

'Please try it, Anne,' encouraged her guidance tutor. 'They have great success.'

'Okay, I will go once.' Which is the only reason she is now sitting in the base on chairs put out in a circle.

'What's your name?' asked the person. 'I am Tania, welcome.'

'TANIA. YOU HAVE GOT TO BE JOKING!' said Anne.

Anne's contrary behaviour when she disagreed with everything was common. Even when she huffed and puffed loudly, Tania recognised the familiar behaviour of this young person.

'Heard you were good. I'm not going to be another one of your statistics, do you hear me?' said a now angry Anne. Tania ignored this and continued.

'Thanks everyone, see you again next week. Remember, you have the number if you wish to have a one-to-one chat over the next week.'

No way was she ever going back – Tania and Tania, a pair of horrors. But curiosity got the better of her the following week. Angry comments were ignored until Anne felt safe and secure in the sessions.

***

Tania was pleased the following week that, as she tidied up, Anne hung back. A one-to-one chat ensued as they put away the chairs. The relief was tangible. Anne's face physically relaxed, she shared that that other bitch Tania purloined Dad, by luring him from his family. 'I thought you just said your parents split up before he met Tania?'

Tears welled, then the steady flow started as she sniffed, wailed, then said resentfully, 'They did,' before she recoiled.

'Would you like to sit for a minute?' said Tania.

Anne nodded and Tania handed her a handkerchief.

'It was not your fault, Anne. Relationships are complex.'

Averting her gaze from the floor, she acknowledged Tania's comment with a nod.

Chapter Nine

That night after speaking to Tania at school, feeling lighter in spirit, Anne phoned Oliver. After she told him what she was doing, he lingered on the line. They both spoke for a while, having reconnected through regular phone calls. Anne began to feel unwell over the summer. Being weaned off painkillers, along with no more parties, was very difficult. This resulted in terrible mood swings. Regression happened once or twice. She enjoyed the woozy, familiar feeling when taking the painkillers in larger quantities than prescribed. It was very hard, yet she remained motivated to quit. The goal became a strong desire, to hear people link their names together again: Oliver and Anne.

Slips made her angry, thinking Oliver would be equally annoyed. On those nights they never conversed. Tonight Anne lifted the receiver of the cream Bakelite rotary dial phone, attached to the kitchen wall. The excitement always started when dialling the numbers, then the connection was made while waiting patiently until the familiar voice said 'hullo'.

'Hullo yourself,' she cheerfully said, before an awkward silence fell between them.

The voice triggered the visualisation of that hand holding the receiver. The pushed-up soft curly hair, exposing his right ear. The familiar sound of his voice brought comfort as they chatted about their day.

Tonight was different.

'Still there?' she asked.

'Mm. What is it, Anne?' he said, irritated. 'You haven't called all week.'

'I know,' she whimpered.

***

Later that night, lying in bed content with a full belly of yummy roasted cheese and tomato, Oliver replayed the conversation.

He had ended all contact over the past few weeks, refusing to engage, asking his mum to answer the phone and tell Anne he was busy studying.

Earlier that evening, his mum had nipped out for milk before making supper. When the phone rang, thinking it may be Gran, he'd answered and the familiar 'Hullo' made his heart jump.

'Oliver, it's me, wait please, I need to see you. Please meet me at our usual spot tomorrow.'

'Why?' he said.

'Please,' she said.

'Okay, Anne, just this once, bye,' he said, distracted by the rumblings in his tummy. Hearing Anne's voice had weakened his resistance, he agreed to meet the next day, on that beautiful autumn day in September.

***

Having been to the chemist a couple of months before, a pregnancy test was handed in. 'Congratulations,' said the cheery voice, 'I'm pleased to inform you the pregnancy test is positive.'

Was it an old wive's tale or could girls actually conceal a pregnancy and deny to their bodies they were pregnant? Anne wondered if this was true as Oliver later said he noticed no change walking towards her.

Anne remained dumbfounded by the cheery woman in the chemist who broke the news, yet knew nothing of the circumstances surrounding this pregnancy. Putting in the test was a trite gesture, expecting it to come back negative, after all her symptoms were down to being weaned off the medication. In feeling so unwell, never once was there any expectation it would be positive; congratulations you are pregnant. These words rang in her ear for some time, while the tears, panic and fear stayed throughout.

The next day, Anne, a small petite girl with long mid-brown hair and round blue eyes full to overflowing with tears, stood close beside the shaken young man. Oliver was taller and lithe in stature with blond hair and jade green eyes. Only seventeen he starts to cry, at nearly sixteen, she steps forward to hug him and then starts to sob uncontrollably.

They are huddled together. Standing in their usual meeting spot near enough to the gates, far enough away from the hustle and bustle of family life; it's late September, the trees are beginning to glow with stunning, rich autumnal colours.

'Why are you crying, Oliver? It's me who has to go through with it.'

'I don't know, I am scared,' he said.

'So am I,' sobbed Anne.

'What will you do?' he asks.

'What will I do? No, Oliver, what will WE do?'

'Nothing, wait,' he said.

'Okay.'

Unbeknown to Anne, at sixteen-nineteen weeks when an unborn baby ingests the sweet amniotic fluid, it takes in larger quantities than if the fluid were bitter.

The next few weeks pass in a blur. Every night they walked and talked as they jointly made plans.

'My gran and grandpa are getting a new couch, I could ask for that,' said Oliver.

'Oliver, where would we put it? We don't have a home.'

'True,' replied the innocent young man. 'I think we could stay with mum.'

'Maybe my mum, although she has the boys who are so noisy.'

Seasonal changes meant it was getting colder. The increased need to wrap up well was necessary to withstand the weather, frost on the trees and a glow from the moon.

'It's strange, Anne, that you can smell the change in weather.'

'I do smell the change, Oliver. It hurts my nose, it stings, constricting my chest, I feel cold to the bone. Shivery, then start coughing.' Oliver then moves closer and wraps his arm around her, and they snuggled close together as one. 'You look like Rudolph.' She touched his cold red nose.

They chuckled, which made them sound so young and frivolous. They enjoyed the moment before having to share their news tomorrow. They had already discussed and picked what they think is the right moment to tell their parents.

Chapter Ten

'I need to go, Tania. The way Morag sounded. I know it's important.'

'As important as me?' pined his new girlfriend.

'You know what I mean,' Dave said.

Going round to the house was sad. It looked so cosy from the outside, the lamps were lit and Morag had good taste with all the matching blinds. A proper family home he wished he was still part of.

As soon as he heard the news, Anne's dad was angry. 'Wait till I see that bloody wee shit.'

'Dad, stop, why are you being like this?' said Anne.

'I didn't want you being with him, he will never amount to much. Single mother, should have known better and stopped you from seeing him. But no, your mother wouldn't hear of it.' Mimicking Morag, he said, '"They may outgrow each other naturally, or maybe not, Dave, maybe she has found her soul mate." Stupid,' he continued, puffing himself up as if he was right. He looked at her with anger in his eyes before saying, 'You clearly still read too many Mills and Boon books.'

Catching her unaware Morag looked dejected, turned sadly away towards Anne, then quickly turned back and said, 'Dave, I am warning you, enough, listen and be quiet. Oliver and his mum are coming here tomorrow.'

Dave was to further regret saying that if Anne married that no good little arse, the son of a PIRATE, it would not last. Well, he was angry, they clearly didn't understand that. The attempt to count to ten was futile, he couldn't stop himself as his temper flared.

'Sit there and shut up, Dave. You are in my house. Don't you dare say another word about Susan and Oliver or you are out of the meeting tomorrow.'

Dave arrived slightly earlier the next evening. Morag guided him straight into the kitchen even though Dave was about to go straight into the living room to 'his seat'. Minutes later Anne answered the door, bringing Oliver and Susan to join the family in the kitchen. The atmosphere is instantly charged negatively with testosterone. Once seated they all looked nervously from one to the other, unsure who would take the lead in starting the difficult conversation.

'Tea anyone?' asked a nervous Morag.

'Yes please,' replied Susan and Oliver in unison.

'What do you take in it?' said Morag.

'Two sugars and milk for both, Mum,' Anne chipped in.

Susan exhaled louder than she intended. Then looked affectionately at Anne and Oliver before starting off the conversation. 'You are both so young.'

The look of disdain from Dave would have curdled milk. He looked from Susan to Oliver, then again from Oliver to Susan. Raised his eyebrows and sighed loudly. Oliver was saddened. His mum looked down at the floor. This angers the young man. 'Are you okay, Mum?'

'Yes, son,' says Susan, trying to sound jaunty.

He knows by Dave's reaction that the previous nights conversation has been discussed, about Susan being a single parent and Dave's disrespect of them.

Morag also knew Dave's reaction and comments the previous night had been passed on. Feeling equally embarrassed towards the visitors, she sighed then said, 'Are you okay, Susan?'

Susan nodded. Morag, distracted, looked awkwardly beyond Susan to Dave who was putting something in the bucket. Morag raised her eyes upwards, revealing her frustration at Dave's comments the previous night. The atmosphere became less emotionally charged by the time Dave sat back down.

'Biscuit anyone?' Anne passed the chocolate digestives round.

'Yes.' Dave reached over and grabbed two, dipped them in his tea, then ate them noisily like a defiant child. He listened yet continued to drink his tea noisily, making no eye contact, appeared insensitive to the situation being discussed. This really upset Morag and Anne. 'There are many options. You don't need to rush in,' said both mums.

Dave sighed loudly, then said, 'Really?' in a sardonic tone.

The conversation naturally ends.

'Another cuppa anyone?'

'No thanks, I need to get home as I have work in the morning,' said Susan.

As soon as the visitors left Morag handed Dave his jacket saying, 'You were purely here as her dad. You couldn't even remember your manners, and your comments last night have clearly been passed on. Goodnight.' She edged him to the door, desperate for him to leave. Anne and Morag would sort this out with or without him.

The meeting for Susan and Oliver felt even more awkward given Dave's reaction.

'Excuse me, Oliver.' She reached over to fill the kettle, he moved from staring aimlessly out the window at his reflection. His mum sighed. 'Oliver, I thought your dad and I would last forever.'

Oliver looked at his mum, the tears flowing gently down her cheeks. Instinctively this made him move forward and hug her. 'Mum, it's alright.'

'Yes,' she says quietly, 'it will be, Oliver. I was always embarrassed, I never set out to be a single parent. Yet Dave thinks it's okay to have a go at us without even knowing us.'

'Mum, don't cry, he is an old fool. No better than us. Look at the mess he has made of his life.'

'I know, Oliver, and I would never say that to him. What makes him think he is better than us? Rejecting us without even knowing us.'

'He is not better than us. Morag and Anne don't think that, which is more important than what that buffoon thinks of us'.

Dave became an outcast from the family that became stronger than ever. Who did not require him at the helm of the ship. He too was lost at sea never to be recovered by his family.

***

The move from being single to a young couple within Oliver's family home went well. Amused, Susan passed the open bedroom door and heard Anne say to Oliver:

'Look at the mess of this room, how can you live like this, Oliver. I am not living in this hovel.'

'Mm,' he said.

'Oliver, you listening to me?' said Anne.

'Yes. Are you saying your hormones are a bit of a mess? That's a shame.'

'MY HORMONES! Why are you saying that?' Tears welled in her eyes.

'Sorry, I was distracted. What were you saying?' He knew by the tone of Anne's voice he'd better give this one his full attention.

'I was saying,' her voice grated with frustration, 'this room needs tidied up.'

Good luck with that one, thought Susan, going downstairs with the dirty laundry from the linen basket on the landing.

A few minutes later, Oliver arrived in the kitchen and took a few bin bags from the cupboard. As he was about to ascend the stairs, he stopped and looked over the banister, saying, 'You will be pleased, Mum. I was thinking we should tidy my room. Put some things to the charity shop. That will make space in my room for Anne.'

'Really, Oliver?'

'Well, not quite like that. Anne is going on about it. I thought it sounded good.' He chuckled.

'I love that girl, she has done in one fell swoop what I have taken … mm let me think … years without success to do.' They both laughed as he continued taking the stairs two at a time.

They spent the rest of the afternoon tidying the room, keeping some of Oliver's toys and knick-knacks, just in case the baby might like them. Anne would have smiled if she hadn't felt so nauseous. Feeling guilty having just moved in, she hoped Susan would not feel upset by this assertiveness, while instinctively knowing the room had to be de-cluttered.

'Next you will be suggesting putting everything up in your mum's loft to take with us once we have a house. Whenever that will be.'

'What a great idea,' he said. 'I suggested that earlier on, Miss Cheeky Chops, you clearly weren't listening.'

Trying to lighten the mood by catching her arms, they wrestled until they both fell on the bed laughing. He kissed her head, and she snuggled into his arm. They stayed there for a while and must have nodded off. When they woke she was feeling less nauseous and more industrious.

'Right, let's get this show on the road. Finish the task in hand. Come on, Oliver.'

It took a few minutes to convince him, yet when they got started it was tidied in no time at all.

'Ask your mum to come up please, Oliver.'

'You ask,' he said.

'Susan,' Anne called from the top of the stairs. 'Do you have a minute?'

'Yes, coming now.'

'My! My! Very pleasing to the eye,' said Susan with a glint in her eye. 'Oliver, how did this happen?'

'Mum, stop, you know fine well how it happened, Fairy-Anne made me.'

They all chuckled and Susan sat on the bed. 'You okay, Anne? I know it's not home, but I do hope you will feel at home here.'

'I do, Susan, thanks very much, we don't know what we would have done without you and Mum.'

'We are always here for you both.'

'Thanks very much.' Anne moved over to Susan. The two women hugged. Oliver smiled, pleased they got on so well. It had been him and his mum for so long. His dad was a pirate, went to sea, drank some rum and never came back. That's how he remembered it.

Chapter Eleven

Baby arrived safe and well a few months later. Mum, Dad, Gran, Grandpa and Susan all huddled round the sleeping baby.

'What a perfect ending. Look at that delightful face,' they all cooed.

'Look at those wee chubby hands,' said Nana Susan when Arianna tried to reach the mobile above her head at around three months.

'Isn't she a wee star,' said Gran Morag. 'I could kiss her and eat her up.'

'Steady, Morag.' Oliver laughed. 'That would be viewed as cannibalism.'

The family were convinced her contentment was due to being spoiled with love. A happy baby who was slightly built and when she started to crawl was off like a shot. She frequently sat up on her hunkers, turned and laughed a toothy grin as they all clapped their hands at her achievements.

'Come on then,' said Anne, lifting the baby. Her outstretched arms raised high above her head, Arianna had quickly learned that when Anne pointed to the ceiling if she lifted her head her mum would tickle under her chin. With squeals of delight, this thrilled both baby and the young mum.

Later came scrambling down from the table, craving independence.

'Will Mum help you?'

'NO,' her youngster replied with fierce concentration to prevent falling over. Once down she ran with gusto into the lounge.

Sometimes the youngster, trying to gain control of her physical skills, jumped off the couch onto the floor. Anne's records would jump and scratch. This meant she put a halfpenny or a penny onto the needle to stop it jumping. Ironically the song playing was 'Jump to the Beat.'

This happy child was a delight to have around. Arianna spent time with extended family and enjoyed wonderful opportunities to play.

When she was old enough, Gran Morag shared tales of when she was young, the love she had for her own grandma, along with passing down family history while baking.

'Do you know, Arianna, I loved to help my gran in the kitchen? The trademark dishtowel was always draped over her left shoulder, becoming a make-do oven glove on many occasions.'

'Aw, Gran, she sounded lovely.'

'She had big brown eyes. Well-nourished skin. Always immaculate. I loved the touch of her hands, they felt soft and endearing. The smell of Oil of Ulay and Tweed perfume still triggers thoughts from days gone by. As a young child I loved to pull a chair over, it was hard to clamber up and stand next to Grandma on the chair. I remember feeling ten-feet tall. I loved being given a saucer along with some homemade pieces of pastry to roll out and place onto the white crockery. Apples spread into the middle, but never too near the edge.

'"Why Grandma?" I would innocently ask. Then affectionately Grandma would say, "You will see, ma darling." Then she'd kiss my adored little face and tap the work surface as a reminder to focus on the apple tart being made. I also remember great precision was required to add the top layer once rolled out. It had to fit over the saucer. Grandma next showed me how to seal the pie with water, which magically stuck the layers together. Fluting the edges took skill, which my young fingers still had to develop. Grandma, on the other hand, achieved perfection. A pastry brush dipped in milk was gently brushed over the top and absorbed into the pastry to eventually glaze the pie as it cooked in the oven.

'I impatiently said within five minutes, "Grandma, is it ready now?" and she'd say, "You will smell when its nearly ready, ma darling."'

'Aw, Gran, that's sweet,' said Arianna.

'Her garden was an outdoor larder with plump red raspberries, only picked when required. The parsley was always the final ingredient added to many pots of soup. Thick stocks of pinkish red rhubarb, trimmed and washed, along with a small circle of greaseproof paper delicately shaped into a cone before being filled with sugar to dip the slightly bitter rhubarb in,' said Morag.

***

When Arianna was with Susan they made and played with gloop and made dough.

'Do you remember the winter walk with the snowmen called Frosty and Freeze?' said Susan on one of Arianna's visits.

'Not really, Nana, tell me,' said Arianna.

'We brought them home then watched them melt on the windowsill.'

'I don't remember,' said Arianna. 'Aw, but I do remember the sandcastles lined up in a straight line, then we watched the tide come in and wash them away one by one.'

'I remember your dad telling me another story. You were given a *holiday penny* from the family. As soon as you got to Arran you saw a toy in the first shop and were desperate to buy it. Your mum and dad tried to dissuade your impulse buy. The toy was duly purchased, along with a warning, all your money was spent, not to ask for any more money all week. "I won't," you said and your dad said you never did. You spent the week playing with the new toy and had the best time ever.'

The family loved when Arianna couldn't work something out. She would look up with big wide eyes and say, 'How come that is?'

***

After Anne finished training as a nursery nurse, it proved very different being a mum. At times feelings of inadequacy overtook logic, and going to the baby clinic and meeting other mums triggered insecurity. Comparing herself and Arianna's development to other children when she really had nothing to worry about. Arianna was loved and bright as a button.

But bedtime was becoming a nightmare.

'Mum, Dad! I NEED a drink of water.'

'One sip, then off to sleep. Night night.'

'One more kiss,' she'd say, holding up her index finger. They'd give her kisses, too many to recount, along with air kisses.

Getting out of bed, she'd say, 'I need this toy,' and get a stuffed animal from the other side of the room.

'You have three already in bed.'

'It's onely (lonely),' said the chancer.

'Quick, in you pop,' said dad or mum to the young bambino. Then when that wouldn't appease the boundary breaker, next came the irrational fear of the actual bed, the spiders, which crawled in during the day and felt like they were tickling all ten toes.

'GO TO SLEEP!'

'I need the toilet.'

While sitting on the toilet, Arianna looked around before becoming the dehydrated philosopher who needed another hug. Anne, bending down, looked into the big wide eyes, the warmest smile exuding from this young scamp, melting her mum's heart.

'Come on, it's way past bedtime. You must go to sleep. Arianna, this must stop you know bedtime is bedtime. Tomorrow night this is not happening again. Its straight to bed without this routine you are trying to create, it's not happening, do you hear me?'

'Mm hhe vuv (love) you, Mum.' Arianna smiled, listening to her mum, not fully understanding her frustration. After all children do not like parents or carers going downstairs and leaving them alone with the midnight beast. Anne's training was of no use in explaining how what is supposed to be a one-hour routine somehow becomes an hour and a half, no matter what time the pantomime starts.

Night after night of the same routine, when one night Oliver looks over at Anne from the mountain of papers on the table, then proceeds to chip in his opinion of the situation.

'Mark my words, she goes down for me no bother.'

'REALLY?' replied an irate Anne.

'You made the rod to break your own back the first time you climbed those stairs and gave into her unreasonable demands.'

'Honestly, Oliver, you have no idea. What if she has no friends at pre-school? What if Arianna is worried about something and needs to tell me?'

'Really, Anne, I can't believe you have fallen for that, and you a nursery nurse.'

'Oliver, how many times do I have to tell you, when I am at home I am a mum not a nursery nurse. And stop being such a pain in the neck. Thinking you know it all, there was only you and your mum who probably did the very same.'

'No, I don't think she did, that's why I turned out as well as this,' he said, rolling his hands up and down over his whole body, trying to bring humour to lighten the situation, quickly realising this was one he had completely mis-read.

Anne, tired, couldn't be bothered listening to this person across the room pontificating and talking nonsense. With an exasperated sigh she left the room, going into the kitchen to start the nighttime routine. The sooner it was done the sooner she could sit down and have a rest.

Oliver tried to speak, however, with both being tired, they watched a bit of TV, had something to eat for supper, then off to bed to do it all again the following day. They both fell exhausted into bed. Oliver studied hard. But it could be hard at times and very demanding as a working mum. Anne didn't mind supporting him to enable his dream of being able to pursue a career as an architect. Papa, Anne's dad, continued to try to be forgiven by being attentive to Anne's little girl. Anne allowed her dad to visit sometimes but their relationship was never the same.

***

When she was old enough Arianna liked being cuddled up with Nana on the settee.

'Tell me again, Nana, about when you were a wee girl in the olden days.'

'I loved the social side of school and chatted away daily to classmates, getting the belt. I remember in Primary 1 I waited in the dinner line to be escorted safely over to the dinner hall. The infant mistress demanded silence. Talking, I never heard the command. The next thing I felt the sting on the back of my legs as the curled-up leather made contact, whipping and hurting my tiny legs. Then the splayed leather recoiled like a snake ready to sting the next victim. It hurt. I did not cry. The next day I tried to convince my dad I didn't want to wear those tights again as they made my legs sore and too warm.'

Arianna said, 'Oh, Nana, that's a shame, you were too young to realise it was not the tights but the belt. I can't believe they were allowed to belt such young children, in fact, any child.'

Chapter Twelve

New baby, new life. As the closing date for UCAS forms was mid-January, it was never submitted. Leaving school, Oliver worked as a temp for the council, then got a full-time job within the planning department. They celebrated when he got his first wage.

'Oh this is a lovely treat,' said Anne, tucking into the shared takeaway meal to celebrate.

'It's great news, this means we don't have to worry so much about money.'

'We will manage, Oliver, we have come through much worse. We will get there, always have and always will.'

***

Adjusting to their new life saw all hopes and aspirations go month after month. Anne saw the dream disappear from his eyes. Late at night they had the same discussions. Maybe uni was something worth considering now. Eventually they made enquiries about the financial sustainability of this. It would be hard. It would be temporary. Unbeknown to them they never truly anticipated the total disruption to their now settled lives. A few years later his application was successful. Uni was very hard for Oliver, and Anne was again frequently irritated with him. Mainly due to having to deal with everything at home along with a demanding toddler, while he studied.

This change in financial status didn't fill him with hope even though Anne was right, they didn't just survive they thrived. Anne went full time to bring in more money. Having reconnected with Hazel and Caroline, the kiss between Oliver and Dee was discussed, where it emerged he had left that night with a sly devious diva.

Anne and Oliver struggled over the years. The young couple drifted apart for a while when their daughter was very young. Oliver studied at university, worked late into the night in the library, then came home for a quick shower and change of clothes, then back to uni. Anne being a good homemaker meant everything ticked along. The longing to see and be with Oliver evoked feelings of loneliness once the wee one was in bed. Mum and Susan were so kind, particularly Susan who never once told Oliver to leave the turbulent relationship and move on. That forged a bond which was to last a lifetime. Anne always bought a little extra on every special occasion or taking both mums flowers. Just because they were so good at helping with Arianna.

After they married, they focused on extending the family. It was sad how things happened. As a couple, they dreamed of having a big family. They tried. She became pregnant but suffered miscarriages. After the first, they both attended the hospital. It wasn't possible to extend the family. The doctor was unable to offer any reasonable explanation, other than perhaps, she could not carry male foetuses.

They cried together over many years for their lost babies. It was hard. They eventually accepted that two became three and there would be no more.

***

Oliver was in the library one day, when Dee approached him.

'WELL HELLO, stranger, how are you,' said Dee, rather loudly.

He looked up as the librarian said, 'Shh,' then pointed to the notice. 'Silence at all times.'

Embarrassed, he quickly closed his books, packed up, then left. Dee followed behind, like a lovesick puppy.

'Oh my goodness, I can't believe it, it's really you, Ollie,' said Dee, who touched his shoulder as he moved back. 'How are you?' she said.

'Good, thanks.'

Then an awkward silence fell between them. He sensed she was annoyed, but was unsure why.

'What have you been up to since I last saw you?'

'Married now, we have a wee girl, Arianna,' he said.

'Who did you marry? Hopefully not that bitch Anne,' she said, then put her hand over her mouth before saying, 'Did I actually say that out loud?'

'You did and I did.'

'Shit that is a real conversation stopper. Can I buy you a coffee as a peace offering?'

'Mm,' Oliver hesitated.

'Come on, it's only a coffee,' she said.

'Okay.'

They had coffee and chatted about how their lives had changed. He found her easy to talk to. He confided that life was very hard, as Anne was irritable a lot of the time. He understood why, yet didn't know what he could do to change things.

'I could come and babysit for you both. It would let you have a night out. Another peace offering for being so tactless, I'm sure Anne has changed over the years. We all have. All grown up now. What are you studying?'

'Architecture. You?'

'Back to do teacher training, at long last, as life got in the way,' Dee said.

'Same for us, I am delighted to be studying now. It would have been easier before Arianna arrived. Sometimes life takes twists and turns.' He checked his watch. 'I better crack on, thanks for the coffee,' he said.

'No problem, you can get me one back,' she said.

'Sure,' he replied, a bit taken aback as this was a peace offering. Once back to the studies everything else was forgotten about.

The next week she sought him out in uni. Dee pretended to bump into him at the café.

'Oh hi, Ollie, we really must stop meeting like this,' she said, standing behind him in the queue.

'I will get this for you, Dee,' he said.

'Oh that's so kind, Ollie. Thanks.'

They sat together and he chatted about the awful nights they were having with Arianna. She was currently unwell. The stress of trying to meet deadlines, juggle family life. He was exhausted.

'Oh you poor thing. Did you ask Anne about babysitting?'

'Forgot,' he said genuinely. 'I will, as a night out could be just what we need. We usually get Mum or Morag to watch Arianna.'

'Someone different could be fun,' she said. A little too desperately, but he never picked up the subtext.

They seemed to meet quite a few times after that. She needed to talk to him. Get a male perspective of something. Oliver began to suspect this was not accidental. He was not comfortable. That day, leaving Dee, he said, 'Dee, I can't keep meeting you.'

She lunged forward and kissed him. He was shocked.

She looked annoyed. 'Ollie, we could still have something, don't you think?'

'NO!'

He left. She stared at him going away from her. Anger bubbled to the surface. She fumed at being rejected again for that little slut Anne.

***

A few weeks later it was early evening, Arianna was tucked up in bed. Anne was distracted while hanging up the washing on the clothes horse.

'The project is really coming together with Liz, Megan and Ben,' said Oliver.

'That's great,' Anne replied, not really listening.

'I met and chatted to Dee in the library. She is there to gain a teaching qualification. We went for a couple of coffees together. Dee remembered you.'

Still distracted as Oliver chatted away, Anne added the odd, 'Oh yes, mm.'

'She asked if I remembered leaving her at the chippy and when I said no, she said "REALLY".'

Still only half listening, Anne was busy thinking about the next night's dinner as well as Arianna's clothes for the next day. Anne gave the conversation no more thought. Until a few nights later, sitting in the kitchen with their usual milky drinks, she put her legs on his knees. They chatted about their day. Which happened less frequently due to Oliver's studies.

He said nonchalantly, 'Remember Dee from school? She was asking for you and was surprised we were still together.'

Anne felt a surge of rage. 'Are you serious, Oliver?'

'What do you mean?'

'Remember when we split up? She was horrible. Hazel told me all about Dee who talked and batted her eyelids at you. Such a bitch. No loyalty. Offered to burn a CD for you. Burnt more than a CD, she burnt her bridges with Hazel.'

'I don't remember.'

'You don't remember! You danced and kissed her, then left with her,' said a frustrated Anne.

'I left her at the chip shop and went home,' he said.

'Be careful round her, in fact, go ahead, go out with her,' Anne screamed angrily. 'I knew it. You have been different recently. Always working, what about last weekend, were you really working all night or out with Dee? Are you really that naïve, Oliver, or plain stupid?'

'What do you mean? We did meet up a couple of times for coffee. She was upset and asked to speak to me. Having some trouble in her relationship.'

'There you go. I am going to bed.' Anne stomped out of the room and upstairs.

Sitting dejected downstairs, Oliver wondered was she being jealous or had he indeed been foolish around Dee? He loved only Anne. He rubbed his hands through his hair. *Oh no, maybe I should have confessed. Dee did try to kiss me. I should go tell her.* He never did, taking the cowardly way out, as Anne was really angry. *I will tell her tomorrow.*

Anne rarely got so angry, the next day she shouted, 'Denise was a bitch at school. Turned her nose up and snubbed people. A very pretentious person who believed she was better than the rest of us. Selfish horrible bitch. YOU KNOW, OLIVER, YOU KNOW VERY WELL, YOU KISSED HER THAT NIGHT AT THE DISCO!' Anne screamed.

'Anne, please, I don't remember kissing her then.'

'Of course you won't. That night, Denise was still trying to get those claws into you and under her spell. Like a wicked witch.' She continued relentlessly, 'Don't you remember I told you at the time, Dee was always the one who was different.' Anne mimicked her tone and actions. 'What Dee wants, Dee gets, probably always has and always will, that's what we all concluded.'

'Oh shit, what have I done?' he said loudly.

Uncharacteristically, they didn't speak for weeks. Anne had gone to her mum's telling her Oliver needed peace and quiet to study.

What he failed to tell Anne was that the particular weekend when he never came home, to gain time and meet the looming deadline, Oliver did meet Dee a couple of times in the uni for coffee. This school friend of Anne's was very upset, needed someone to talk to. Oliver now realised how foolish he'd been.

Home alone, the house was so quiet and there was no milk in the fridge. *I could phone Anne, not a good option. Phone Mum, not a good idea.* Going outside, Oliver felt the cold and saw the reflection of his breath. He wanders to visit Grandpa, full of melancholy. Going into Gran and Grandpa's house, it's warm and cosy with the smell of lentil soup on the cooker – hopefully no Brussel sprouts in it this week.

'Oliver, what a lovely surprise! Come in, lad, soup's just made ready for the week.'

'Thanks, Gran.'

Nodding towards the living room, she said, 'Your grandpa is in there.'

Going in, Oliver greeted Grandpa with a hug. He beamed and smiled, turning off the radio that was playing Tommy Scott and the band.

'Oh your grandpa was just listening to the da de da de da music. Singing away like a linty.' Gran smiled, then raised her eyes upwards. 'Glad you popped in, Oliver, you saved me from my excruciating weekly experience.'

'Don't listen to Gran,' Grandpa joked. 'Don't you know singing is a stress buster?'

'It may be to you, but for the people listening, it is very stressful.' Gran chuckled. They smiled affectionately at each other.

He liked visiting and remembered he must come around more often. *Life is busy, mental note to self: must make more effort, they won't be here forever.*

The soup was delicious. Oliver is unusually quiet. Both grandparents put it down to studying too hard. They ask after Anne and Arianna.

'Your wee family well?' asked Grandpa.

'Yip, I am busy with uni work, so they have gone to her mum's for a couple of days to give me peace to study. Great to see you both,' Oliver said affectionately on his way out.

After he left his grandparents chatted.

'Oliver looks a bit glum. Whatever it is they will work it out. That look is not just uni work.'

'Yes,' said Grandpa.

'We will know soon enough. I'll speak to his mum if need be. Life will be hard for them as a young couple and their baby, trying to juggle so many demands.'

On the way home, Oliver stopped to buy some milk. The lonely walk, dreading the empty house, brought an acute sense of sadness. *How could this have happened?* thought a dejected Oliver. Having never kissed Dee, it was she who had kissed him.

He replayed the scene in his head.

'What are you doing?' he asked as he refuted Dee's advances.

'Anne doesn't need to know, does she? Come on, Ollie, you know we have always had something special.'

'No, we haven't,' Oliver had replied, baffled; the implication of a quick fling stunned him. 'Get lost, Dee,' he'd said, in no uncertain terms. Along with an expression of disgust. When Anne got angry it dawned on him how foolish he had been. He would be lost without Anne and Arianna in his life.

Arianna is staying the night with Susan. The phone ringing breaks the silence. Mum's voice echoed through the phone. 'Hi, love, I have a wee one here wanting to say goodnight.'

'Nnigt.'

'Night night, Arianna, sleep well, baby girl.'

'She is off, love, speak soon.'

'Bye, Mum.'

Back wallowing in self-pity, Oliver drank his tea, the unusual stillness of the house eerie. The more he wallowed the angrier he got. Anne and Arianna leaving reminded him that his dad was never around. His mum was devastated and hurt at the time.

He pens a note to Anne.

Anne,

Please forgive me. What an idiot I have been. Have I been a daydreamer while you have always been the sensible one since we got married? You are my best friend and soulmate, we are a team. I can't do this without you. Please come home with Arianna. I am so sorry. I promise to be a better husband to you. I know I never tell you, but I am so proud of you, turning your life around. At college getting between 80-100 in your final paper and passing with distinction was a great achievement, Anne. I love you so much. I went to see Gran and Grandpa. You are a great mum to Arianna. Please come home, I miss you both.

Lots of love,

Ollie xx

He found an envelope, put the letter inside and sealed it, then wrote her name with his left hand (so his mum wouldn't recognise his writing), headed back out and walked to his mum's. He tossed and turned all night, wondering if Anne got the letter. The next day, he hardly took in any information at uni. Exhausted, he headed home for another lonely night.

Unlocking the door, he entered to the familiar scent of his family.

'DADDY DADDY DADDY!' said the excited toddler as she ran towards him.

'Oh, baby girl, hi,' said Oliver, snuggling into his little girl's neck.

'Hi,' Anne said in a flat voice.

'Hi,' said an equally quiet Oliver.

It takes some time for wounds to heal.

Chapter Thirteen

The girls met in town outside one of the shops. They all looked relaxed, raring to get the celebrations underway. Patiently waiting for the fashionably late Anne to arrive.

'There she is,' said Hazel, waving to the approaching figure hurrying along the road.

'Sorry I'm late, girls, Arianna always senses when I am trying to get out and won't go to bed.'

'Never mind, you are here now,' they all chipped in as they hugged Anne.

The girls linked arms before going into the local Chinese restaurant, for the usual celebratory meal for their respective birthdays.

It's the 10th September and the girls are out to celebrate Hazel's birthday. They go out on the 10th December to celebrate Caroline's birthday. The 21st January to celebrate Anne's birthday and, when Anne was stuck in the house not getting out much, they added the 17th June, Oliver's birthday. It became a standing joke that they celebrated his birthday while he babysat.

A devious and adventurous plan was hatched. The three girls giggled and giggled.

'Oh come on, Ollie, you know we won't go out on the day. We would just like to have another wee sneaky night at your expense,' added Hazel, who cackled at her own joke as they all laughed and collapsed in a heap on the couch. Oliver, now used to this when the girls were together and it got hysterical, shook his head and thought *what are they doing?*

It took Hazel a long time to tell Anne about the night when Dee made a play for Oliver. As a loyal person she found it hard to comprehend how immoral Dee actually was. Even the very words 'all is fair in love and war' were shallow and mean. Anne was so annoyed.

'Bitch.' Then added, 'I hope Dee gets her just desserts.'

They all talked about it over dinner, then again at the dancing.

'What are you talking about?'

'Oh, Caroline, she will get her comeuppance.'

'Ah okay.' They laughed affectionately at Caroline who then said, 'What, just desserts?'

'Oh nothing, Mrs Literal,' joked Hazel. 'Bet those wee chops are now salivating for a wee toffee pudding.'

'So funny!' Caroline smiled.

After school, the friends had gone their separate ways. Hazel started working in the bank and would visit Anne, Oliver and baby Arianna for dinner after work. Caroline worked in a record shop on a Saturday in the local shopping centre, until an opportunity presented itself. A position became vacant to work for a local newspaper, a section reporting on all aspects of the arts which, with her particular passion for music, soon proved to be the dream job.

'Guess what, girls? Who do you think is at uni with Oliver?' After a pause she revealed, 'DEE!'

Shocked, they all said, 'NO WAY!'

'Mm.' Anne nodded, before going into a tirade. Recounting the argument they had had over Oliver actually meeting and kissing her.

'What a horror. Once a chameleon always a chameleon, better watch out, Anne,' said Caroline.

'Seriously, who does that to someone who was a friend?'

'DEE!'

'Well, you know what Freud would say …' said Caroline.

'What?' asked Hazel.

'Freud's theory works explicitly here,' said Caroline.

'What are you talking about?' said Hazel.

'Mark my words, id, ego and superego are all at work here. She will get her claws into him one way or another,' said Caroline, moving her head up and down like a mad professor.

They all laughed hysterically at the absurdity.

A worried Anne said, 'Is she just one of those bad apples?'

'One bad apple don't spoil the whole bunch, girls,' hollered Hazel, moving her hand round the table at Anne and Caroline, then herself.

'What other possible explanation would there be for doing that? Particularly after so long.'

'What Dee wants, Dee gets.'

'Indeed, Anne, sad but true,' said Hazel.

'Anyway, moving on. Hazel, how have your birthday capers turned into this?' said Caroline affectionately and they chuckled.

Then shouted, raised their glasses and started singing, 'Dee Dee who the … is Dee?' to the tune of 'Alice', then chattered away the hours.

Chapter Fourteen

Where did it all go wrong? How did it all go wrong? Arianna's change was slow, a bubbly happy child who appeared to go through all the normative developmental stages. It wasn't as if one night she went to bed a child, then the next morning woke up all sulky with all the teenage angst.

Coming home from school she followed the usual routine, school bag under the stairs, a look in the fridge, before going upstairs to change out of her school clothes.

As the change was gradual, Anne more often found the need to repeat instructions. 'Arianna, please hang your school clothes up on the coat hanger. Remember, the dirty ones go straight into the laundry basket,' Anne said, observing the messy room as she passed.

'I will. Give me time,' said the sullen teenager.

'Okay, love,' responded Anne, who retreated even though there was a pile of clothes on the chair.

Arianna crawled into bed for a nap after school, and, when Anne or Oliver called her for tea, there was no response. They took turns going upstairs where an exhausted 'I will get up in a minute' became the now usual response.

'Are you okay, love?'

'MUM, stop!'

Sitting together waiting on their daughter to join them at the table, a sense of trepidation crept in for Anne. She began to panic, given her own history. Oliver was unable to relate to this. Anne knew how trauma can change young lives and did not want this for their little Arianna. As a family they would get through anything. After all she did.

The exhausted teenager eventually did come to the table, sitting now with one hand on her head. Before moving the food around the plate aimlessly.

'You know, both Gran and Nana asked for you today, why not pop by on your way home tomorrow?'

'I will,' she replied, although she never did. 'Can I go now?' said the two peas and one chip full teenager.

'Yes, please put your plate in the kitchen. Watch, Arianna, those peas are about to tumble off the plate.'

'Hold it properly,' instructed her dad.

'Ohhhh,' huffed their daughter.

'Oliver, I'm really worried,' said the frenetic mother, the rise of panic in her voice did not subside, even after voicing her concerns. 'Oliver, can you speak to her?' said Anne.

'Yes,' said Oliver.

An hour later, Anne asked, 'Did you speak to her?'

'Anne, will you give me time?' said the frustrated dad.

'You are unbelievable,' said the irritated mum. Becoming more and more concerned that this may be something other than teenage angst.

The constant questioning irritated both. 'Just give me a break, I am tired,' said the now also irritated daughter.

They kept doing all the things caring parents do. They continued to worry about her. 'What if she is being bullied, Oliver?'

'Anne, surely we would know.'

'How would we know?'

Anne scoured the internet and every resource she could think of for help. Reading through testimonials from young people, feelings of hopelessness started to consume Anne. Nothing could happen to their beautiful girl, given how hard it had been for them and the extended family.

Speaking to both Morag and Susan, both told Anne not to worry too much, that being a teenager brings about changes to all young people.

This natural developmental stage may have been the case for Arianna, if only she had spoken to either of her parents instead of clicking that button.

While they still worried, they settled and life appeared as normal as it can be with a teenager in the house.

Arianna would suddenly appear downstairs, at bedtime. As if it was early morning, making toast. Eating chocolate and anything else sweet she could find in the cupboard. Her parents would try to start a conversation but it quickly turned into a challenge. If they said black, she said white, there appeared to be no grey in their lives. It was either right or wrong. Even in trying to appease the irrational thoughts of their little darling, nothing worked.

'Why are you looking at me like that?'

'Like what?' said Dad.

'Oh never mind,' said Arianna before running upstairs crying.

Other times Arianna sulked or looked at Anne, then said, 'Stop staring at me, Mum. What is it?'

After each outburst, going back into her bedroom, feelings of guilt rose that consumed the emerging young woman. She loved her mum and dad who were good people. Therefore, Arianna couldn't understand why they irritated her so much. The tears of frustration soon spilled over again.

***

Life continued to be up and down for all of them. With the passing of time the worried parents spoke again to Morag and Susan, who both asked their granddaughter to come for a wee sleepover. They each hoped to rekindle memories of how it used to be when Arianna was a young girl. Movie nights and snacks galore.

'I will, Gran.

'I will, Nana.' Arianna never did.

The months passed. Oliver was now becoming equally concerned, as Anne was not settling so perhaps her intuition was right. They became hyper vigilant to no avail.

One day before Arianna got home, Oliver said, 'Should we look in her room, Anne, to see if we can find out anything?'

'No, that's not right, Ollie. I don't think we should.'

'Me neither, I was just testing you.'

Anne looked over, moved towards him and pretended to push him. They cuddled and laughed before they kissed. Their fears relaxed, they still thought life was as good as it gets with a teenager in the house.

Unbeknown to them Arianna had clicked the button, not because she was unhappy at home. Rather it was to discard the title of being known as a 'goody two shoes' at school. The posts at first were friendly, asking if her mum still saw Hazel and Caroline. She felt a sense of emotional security. Her new friend knew things about her that only someone who was familiar to the family would know. Did her gran still live near the park? Did Susan still work for the same company?

'Yes and yes,' she typed. Then for other questions, she became inventive in the text. Uncharacteristically, a bit rude or cheeky, so her new friend Belinda did not think or suspect she was a mummy or daddy's girl.

It was sometime later that Belinda dropped the bombshell about her dad.

'You know your dad kissed my mum when they were at uni together?'

Shocked by this, Arianna was convinced there was no way this was true. Her mum and dad were solid. Always had been, always would be. *They have been together long before Mum found out she was pregnant with me,* thought Arianna. They had no secrets. She was from a caring, loving family. They lived with Gran before I was born. They loved going to Nana's for dinner and seeing the boys. Yes, they had had hard times, but the strength of the family had got them through. Family is everything, that's what she was brought up to believe.

Chapter Fifteen

Arianna's life over the next few months became very chaotic. Living two lives, the first was gradually replaced from loving daughter, to sulky teenager. The other persona seeped in and permeated her very soul.

Ping, ping, ping. 'Hi, Ari, remember when you go out tonight to have a fag.'

'But I don't smoke,' said the innocent teenager.

'Just try it. Ask someone for one, see if you like it.'

'Why?' said Arianna.

'Because it will help you get accepted,' said her new best friend.

The doubt niggled away at Arianna. An innocent girl, from a close family, this type of behaviour was alien to her.

Later that night, Baz handed out cigarettes to the group. Arianna took one. They all laughed as she spluttered. It tasted awful. She let it burn, then extinguished it soon after.

Ping ping ping. This went on and on. It was relentless.

'Tonight take some alcohol with you.'

'Why? I won't be able to do that,' said Arianna, frightened.

'Who gave you the fag? Ask him to go into the shop for you. Look at what the others drink and get that.'

The youngster duly complied.

The next request was the most outrageous suggestion to date.

'Sleep with a couple of the boys. They will be so impressed, Ari. You will be well accepted, be one of the gang.'

The following weekend, she bought more alcohol, then did as her online pal suggested. It did not feel good. She was scared. She was unsure. She complied. Arianna reported back after each task. Her friend was extremely pleased, giving her ongoing praise and encouragement. In some ways, she wondered, if feeling uncomfortable was due to being protected by the ever loving family she was part of.

It went on and on, week after week. The continual ping, ping, ping of the phone kept her awake, late into the night.

'Morning, Arianna. Oh you look tired, love. Are you feeling okay?' said mum one morning.

'STOP going on, Mum,' said the sulky, stroppy teenager.

'I am only making an observation, young lady. DO NOT SPEAK TO ME LIKE THAT.'

'MUM. I asked you to stop.'

'NO, Arianna, you didn't. You were cheeky and rude,' said Anne.

Later that evening, while Arianna was voluntarily imprisoned in her room, Anne told Oliver she was worried.

'I am sure she is okay, Anne.'

'I hope so, Oliver,' replied his concerned wife.

This went on for months. Then her parents noticed a change in her pallor. The following morning they heard her being sick in the bathroom. Arianna was convinced and claimed she had an upset stomach from something she had eaten. The following few weeks saw a pattern emerge. Both parents were now gravely concerned.

'I am making an appointment with the doctor, Oliver, this can't go on. She is weakened and looks awful.'

'Yes, I think so, Anne. Do you want me to come as well?'

'No, I will take her,' replied the concerned mum. Never once did they suspect she may be pregnant. Once this was confirmed, they were shocked. Given their own history, neither could believe how naïve they'd been with Arianna.

The doctor asked Arianna to provide a urine specimen.

'When did you last have sex?' said the doctor. The teenager went pale and put her head between her knees. Her mother felt like doing the same, however remained composed.

'Are you sure, Doctor? Are you absolutely sure?' said the stunned mum.

'Yes, I am, I have detected a hormone only present in pregnant women. There is no other way this is presented by the body,' said the doctor to the two shocked people he now faced.

'I will make a referral to the nurse, who will start a plan to support you throughout. They will also give you advice on all your options, Arianna,' the doctor said sensitively.

Once home, Anne called, 'OLIVER. OLIVER. OLIVER. COME DOWN PLEASE.'

He came running down the stairs. Arianna passed him, going straight to the toilet. She locked the door, then cried silent tears.

'Anne, what is wrong with Arianna?' he asked his visibly distressed wife.

'I think you better sit down, Oliver,' said Anne.

He did, then she said, 'Arianna is pregnant. Oliver, please don't cry.'

He could not speak, when he did all he said was, 'How?' She got up and went over. They both hugged and cried. 'What happened to our baby?' he cried.

'Our baby is broken, Oliver, and we did not see it. How could we have let his happen?'

'Shsh, we are both to blame. We've been so stupid. You were right, Anne, to be worried. I am so sorry,' he said through tears.

'It wasn't your fault either, Oliver.'

'How could this have happened? How did we not suspect anything?'

They both sat in stunned silence the rest of the night.

Arianna was unable to speak to her parents. She stayed in her room. Both parents were very aware shouting at Arianna was futile.

The house was stunned into silence. They all went about their business for the first week like zombies.

Arianna shielded her 'best friend online'. Taking full responsibility for the mess she had now created.

'Arianna, come on, we need to go, the appointment is in thirty minutes.'

The sloth-like figure came down the stairs, eyes staring downwards. Head down in shame, the broken-spirited teenager accompanied her mum to the surgery. The nurse was very helpful, going over all of the options for Arianna.

'Take time to think about it, Arianna, about what is best for you. Do you have any thoughts?' asked the nurse.

'Don't know,' she whispered.

Once home, Oliver and Anne said they would help Arianna if she wanted to keep the baby. The new-mum-to-be was terrified by all of the options. The weeks passed and they did talk, but it was painfully awkward, down to Arianna's protection of her online friend.

'Who made you do this?' asked both parents at different times.

'I can't,' said their daughter.

'Who is the dad?' mum asked sensitively. 'Are you in a relationship with him?'

'No,' whispered her embarrassed daughter.

The decision was reached that the baby would come into the family. The pregnancy was difficult, morning sickness, then tiredness. Arianna carried the baby very low. As a result, she had a lot of pain walking.

'Mum, mum come quick.'

Anne knew right away baby was on the way.

'Oliver, get the car we need to go to the hospital.'

Baby Toby arrived safe and well. He was welcomed by all the family. Arianna did not bond very well with him. Anne and Oliver did. This resulted in them being more involved than they had anticipated. Anne encouraged Arianna. The pattern which emerged inadvertently meant Arianna often behaved like the 'big sister' not the mum.

'Give her time,' said Susan on the phone one evening.

'You two are coping so well. I feel sure Arianna will make the transition,' said Morag.

'I hope so,' said Anne on a visit to her mum. Eating a big slice of Madeira cake and a cup of tea, then said, 'This is delicious.'

'Try not to worry, love, look at you and Oliver, life turned out well for you both.'

'You are right, Mum. Better get Toby back home,' said the young grandmother who snuggled the baby close. Both women kissed him, and Anne gently put him in the pram, ready for the return journey home.

Chapter Sixteen

I t was so hard for Anne and Oliver after it happened. Their rooms like shrines to them both. Sitting exactly as they had been left, all those years ago. Until you go through something like that, you can never truly appreciate how you would react.

Arianna's situation was a painful lesson for them all. Living daily with regret tortured both Anne and Oliver with thoughts of *if only this had been shared.*

'Oliver, how I wish we had just told her.' Anne lamented as they cuddled in bed each night.

'Anne, how were we to know?'

'We should have known.' Anne would become so restless she had to get back up and go downstairs. Some nights Oliver followed her downstairs, other times he was asleep by the time she left the room.

In the morning, Anne was often found sleeping on the settee with a cover draped over her. Oliver would reach down and kiss her in peaceful slumbers.

'Hi,' said his sleepy wife.

'Hi, love, why didn't you wake me if you couldn't sleep? I would have come down with you.'

'I'm angry, Oliver, we never saw it.'

'How could we, love? She was a teenager.'

'WE SHOULD HAVE!' Anne wailed.

'Come here.'

'NO. LEAVE ME, OLIVER.'

They agonised for hours and hours over what happened in third year. It began with the marked change when their baby girl became a sullen teenager. They'd put it down to hormones. Then in fifth year going off the rails at exactly the same age as Anne. This tormented the young mum, who constantly questioned how this was possible, was history repeating itself? Had the prescription pills Anne took left indelible traces in Arianna's DNA? After everything they had come through, Oliver's success meant nothing to them without their daughter.

Anne and Oliver *did* hold back information as they firmly believed it was for the right reasons. As things had changed positively for them all, they saw no need to share this information with Arianna, they were not trying to hide anything. That short period of time in their history, paled into insignificance given the support and strength of their family. Yet in her fifth year of school and beyond, the life of their beloved daughter and grandson changed forever. They were all devastated.

Anne lived with the constant regret. Some nights Oliver would say, 'Come on, let's go out for a walk,' and they'd wrap up and cuddle in just like when they were younger. They found when they walked and talked, as they had done so many years before, it was less cathartic this time around with no resolution in sight.

'I will never forgive myself,' said Anne.

'I'm sorry, Anne, I should have listened to you.'

Grieving the loss of their daughter for years meant different stages of loss and grief, sometimes together as a couple. While at other times it pulled them miles apart. Heartbroken, they eventually accepted it had been Arianna's choice to walk away. Devastated it felt like a death in the family, without ever knowing if their darling girl had died.

Daily calls to the police station, desperate that someone would give them the answer that she was going to come home, gradually faded.

'Please, put out a national alert, officer,' Anne pleaded.

The police did call on them at home, to personally deliver the final response, which devastated them both. 'Sorry, Madam, we can't do that as we have found your daughter. However, she does not wish to return.'

'Can you pass on a message please?' whined the distressed mother.

'No,' said the sensitive police officer 'Your daughter has been in touch and does not wish to return.' The family were left with no choice but accept Arianna did not want to come home.

Even the police request to return Toby was also rejected. The papers were already signed, putting their beloved grandson into long-term foster care. Arianna left the local area, having convinced social services of an unhappy home life. Oliver and Anne lost all contact.

***

For years the house felt empty. A veil of sadness suppressed all life inside. It ebbed and flowed back and forward. The guilt was terrible, irrational and obtrusive even if they laughed at something on television. The silent tears flowed till her husband said, 'Look, we did our best.'

Anne was convinced Arianna had not taken prescription drugs, after all, every mum would know, wouldn't they? Doubts niggled at Anne, what if Arianna had done so and they never knew? Tortured thoughts meant agonised nights, weeks and sometimes months in the early days after they both left.

'Do you think things could have been different, Oliver?' cried his wife.

'Anne,' he said, bereft. 'No one would ever have been able to predict this outcome.'

It took years to accept this. In the early days they both constantly wished that it could have been so very different. Eventually they rationalised together, they had to let it go. The agony consumed all their waking hours. The social shame was terrible. Morag and Susan regularly told Anne, 'You did everything you could have done.'

One day the women met at their favourite place. The ambience previously used to comfort Anne. The open fire, the warm glow of lights strategically placed. The brickwork was that of an old cottage. The low ceiling, the wooden chairs softened with plump cushions. They spent hours here over the years. Enjoying family chat and beautifully crafted food. Today Morag noticed her daughter's peaky appearance and knew it had been a hard week.

'How are you doing, Anne?'

'Not great, Mum. With Arianna's birthday approaching, it's so hard.'

'We know,' said both mums, touching Anne affectionately, as a way of comfort.

'I still feel I should have known better.'

'How could you have known, Anne?' said Morag.

'I went off the rails.'

'Aw, you mustn't do that to yourself again, Anne,' both women encouraged Anne to remember 'your past does not have to be your present'. They were extremely proud of the progress this kind, caring person had made by growing into the wonderful young woman before them. They all knew the truth, and as a family they stuck together. They hadn't let any of the gossip bother them.

'I know it hurts, Anne,' said Susan sympathetically. 'However, remember, my darling,' she said, looking into the sad, overwhelmed eyes, which were full of guilt, 'as the old saying goes: today's news wraps tomorrow's chips. Our family story became a seven-day wonder. Yet we know the pain lasts a lifetime.'

'Thanks, Susan.' Anne touched both mums' hands. 'You're both right, let's celebrate Arianna.'

'Here's to you, Arianna, wherever you are. We love you and miss you every day.' They clinked their glasses together. 'To our girl.'

As they were leaving, Anne said, 'Thank you both. I'm glad we did this.'

Chapter Seventeen

All the way through school Denise was a subtle bully who took great pride in making people feel small. She was frequently heard saying cruel things.

'Look at her hair. Who are you looking at, you black get?' she said to one African American girl. This girl looked away offended and considered telling the teacher, but as no one else heard, to save any embarrassment, the girl stayed quiet.

'YOU DIDN'T, did you really?' exclaimed Hazel, open-mouthed, so shocked she could not speak.

Denise, pointing to both sides of her nose with a mean smile, said, 'I will deny I told you, if you dare tell anyone.'

She previously gloated to Anne about the time she put a compass pointing upwards on a girl's chair, who then sat on it and it punctured her skin, while *Denise* laughed. Anne too was open mouthed and shocked to hear such cruelty.

'Tell anyone, Anne, and I will tell them about you when you took those pills, remember for the sore arm you had?' Denise cackled. She was as wily as a fox and never seemed to get caught.

At school, Anne, Caroline and Hazel soon began to see her true colours. They struggled to remain friends with this person who appeared to pick fights, daily, with other less able students.

Six months after the school disco, they were standing together at lunchtime and the wily fox stopped to gloat and said, 'You little swots will be glad to know I am leaving school today,' brandishing her leaving certificate in front of them. Then, head in the air, walked on, turned and put her middle finger up at them.

'She is truly horrid,' said Caroline.

'Agreed,' said the others. 'Good riddance to bad rubbish.'

Denise secured employment in the local shop where she continued to be mean to elderly customers, then pretended to be funny. These comments were denied when the owner overheard what was being said.

'Hurry up and get your stuff, I have a queue waiting, you old fuddy duddy.'

The tearful employee insisted, 'I never said that. He is a liar, hearing aids in so probably didn't hear me say, "Mr Duddy, please take your shopping, take your time, I can wait."'

The owner was suspicious. As a result he never mentioned to Denise when, some time later, he installed CCTV cameras as children were stealing the stock.

The owner was serving this day. 'Hi, how are you today, Mrs Bacca?' he said.

'Good, but I was going to tell you something. My husband said I should let it go as you are such a good man.'

'What do you mean?'

'That one over there, you have working for you, is it Miss D? I was disgusted, thought I couldn't lip read, said that I was an old black get.'

'I offer my profuse apologies, please take this as I am not happy about that,' he said, handing Mrs Bacca a box of chocolates.

'No need to give me these. I just thought you would want to know,' replied the customer.

'I am so glad you did tell me, leave it with me.'

He'd only given Denise the job in the first place due to feeling sorry for the young waif. The dismissal instantly improved customer relations.

A pattern soon emerged. She moved from job to job, worked in a factory, then another shop. Being driven, Denise soon began to study at university part time, this was where she met Oliver for coffee and kissed him. When she challenged a lecturer about the grades awarded for her assignment, arrogance overtook, and she walked out of the class as the lecturer would not amend and upgrade her paper.

'You can stick your course where the sun doesn't shine. I know that was full marks,' she raged, then banged the door as she left.

The shaken lecturer dismissed the class early and reported this to her superior. Denise was asked to attend a meeting, but never did. A couple of years later, Denise returned to a different university to gain the desired teaching qualification she still hungered after.

On graduation day Bobby looked aghast as she kissed the certificate.

'That's good, Denise.'

'Is that all you can say, you twat? No ambition that's your problem, pal,' she raged. 'I will make it to the top, Bobby.'

'Denise, I thought we were going to start a family?'

'Are you stupid, I have just qualified and don't want bogged down with a brat.'

'Please don't say that. I thought we agreed.'

'NAW, pal, you agreed. Did I ever say OH THAT'S A PLAN, BOBBY, did I?' she shouted.

They never recovered from her mean revelation, which quashed Bobby's dream.

The power surge Denise felt was intoxicating, and with a desire to maintain this power, came a driven need to study course after course after course, having secured that dream job as a teacher.

'Bobby, away out to your hut I'm trying to study.'

But, before he could finish, she flicked her hand and dismissed him, waiting till he left.

Sometime later, Denise secured a promoted post. She felt the thrill tingle every nerve in her body when sitting behind the desk separating her from the minions, where the edge of the desk created a boundary.

The newly appointed janitor was asked to put the new name plate on the door.

'Morning, Miss, just here to change the name plate,' said the cheery voice.

'Make it quick, I have work to do,' came the curt reply.

'Quick as I can,' the dejected janitor replied.

This school had a lot of caring, dedicated staff. This irked the newly promoted member of staff, a constant stream at the door and ongoing requests for help frustrated her. With a feigned smile, she thought, *Piss off, can't you see I am busy?* Yet what she said in reality was, 'Hi what's your problem? Okay, let's work out a solution.' But when observant staff and pupils discussed their plights, they all quickly saw Denise's eyes glaze over as the pretend interest disappeared out the open window. The power-driven individual climbed the promotional ladder, securing three different positions in quick succession. Becoming head teacher gave Denise an even more heightened thrill. The exhilarated power was compounded with feelings of being 'punch drunk'. Her heart and head pounded to the beat of 'Eye of the Tiger' being played on the radio. Revelling in these feelings of power, the flashback to playing schools as a child brought a wicked smile across her face again.

Sitting at this new desk she asked once again, 'Are you going to be long?' as the janitor was changing the name plate.

'Quick as I can.'

Once finished, she rose to admire her name on the door before softly kicking the door closed with the back of her foot. Back at her desk, she put her feet up and swirled round on her chair to admire the view, then smirked again. The sense of pride made this scene look almost identical to Melanie Griffith's character in *Working Girl* when she looked out over Manhattan, having secured the job of her dreams. The only difference was that Melanie Griffith had been the underdog, overpowered by Sigourney Weaver's character. This underdog's character had triumphed in the end. Denise on the other hand, became even more power crazy and was never held to account. Nothing seemed to stop her.

She had made it. Sitting in her office, she reflected back. She married once to a loser who constantly refused to go for promotions at work. She tried every way to make him go after that top job unsuccessfully. She basked in the thrill of the perceived prestige, even bought him clothes or filled in the application forms. Equally adamant, Bobby would not comply. He refused to be pushed, and never once went to any of the many interviews he was selected to attend. Completely satisfied at the level of his current job, meant *Denise's* frustration grew so strong that eventually they parted and divorced. Denise was unperturbed at being alone as it allowed more undisturbed hours for her passion, work. Her ex remarried and they had four children, two girls two boys. Apparently they're as happy as the days are long with no driven desire to go for promotions, unlike Denise.

When Bobby left, thoughts of *great, I don't have to justify, why I want to be the best head in the area* consumed every waking hour for Denise. Work, work, work, sometimes forgetting to eat, while other nights falling asleep at the laptop, then waking with a start, as soon as another idea entered her head. Quick coffee and a cigarette, then work again, late into the night. The thrill it gave continued to pump through her veins. Now she even considered piloting weekend work with staff on a rotation of five over 7, till the local authority said absolutely not. Denise banged the computer lid down after reading the refusal email. Once she calmed down she opened it back up, sending a fast response. She, again, pleaded the case with the spreadsheet of why this was a pilot worth further consideration. It was again denied with no further explanation.

Denise, seething, walked around the office then moved over to the computer. Pulled up old emails, reading the refusal again and again, letting the anger rise and spill over, some unlucky individual was about to get the wrath of her tongue.

Then for some reason she went onto one of her social networking sites, and there was Anne smiling back. Still happily married to Oliver, they had little Arianna who was the apple of their eye. It caused a reaction and the past came flooding back. 'That bitch, Anne,' she said, talking to herself. 'I remember that one, what a loser back then, now look at the happy family grinning like Cheshire cats. I bet its "Oh Oliver this, Oliver that". He would have gone out with me, I know he would have, then that bitch came back into the picture. Maybe I will get in touch with her and put her straight.' A wicked smile crossed Denise's face. *What a wonderful idea, maybe, just maybe.*

Chapter Eighteen

The night out had been planned for weeks. They were both so excited. They had not been out together since Toby arrived.

'Remember, love, Dad and I are going out next week,' said Anne.

'Mmm,' said Arianna.

'Do you want me to ask Gran or Nana to come round and be with you and Toby?' asked Oliver.

'No, it's okay,' said Arianna, much brighter than she felt.

'Okay, if you decide you want some company let me know, will you?'

'Anne, do you think she will be okay being alone? Maybe we should just cancel,' said Oliver. He now sounded very unsure.

'We have to trust her, Oliver. I feel sure Arianna will ask us if she wants company.'

Their daughter knew her pal would help her. She was on social media all the time. As soon as Arianna went online, she could see the green icon, saying she was live at that time. Belinda will help her with baby Toby when Mum and Dad go out. She felt sure given how friendly they were.

That night the house smelled of perfume and aftershave. Oliver and Anne came out of their room, looking vibrant, young and happy. Arianna said affectionately, 'You both look really nice.'

'Thanks, love, are you sure you will be okay?' said a slightly nervous Oliver. He had struggled to recover after telling Anne that Arianna was okay, before they found out she was pregnant with Toby.

'I'm sure, Dad. Go and have fun, you and Mum need a night out,' said his only daughter.

'Aw thanks, love, we certainly do.'

They left the house. Both huddled close together as they had done, many years ago. It felt strange going out tonight.

'I am a bit nervous, Oliver, are you?'

'Yes, a bit, I feel a bit uneasy, don't know why.'

'Probably because we have been couch potatoes for forever!'

They laughed and talked as they walked to the venue. Once inside all sense of fear dissipated. They danced and laughed the whole night. What a fabulous much-needed night out they had.

'Will we walk home or get a taxi?' asked Oliver.

'A taxi, my feet are so sore after all that dancing.'

Oliver went to the payphone in the hall and called for a taxi.

'Ten minutes, love. The driver will come in and call our name,' said Oliver.

Leaving the venue, the cold air hit them both as they chuckled like two frivolous teenagers. They both felt very relaxed after the night.

The taxi dropped them outside the house.

'Shh,' said Anne loudly.

'Shh yourself, you are shouting, thinking you are being quiet, Anne.'

'NO, NO, NO,' said Anne loudly, trying unsuccessfully to sound quiet.

'Anne, quiet, you will wake the house.'

'Okay,' said Anne, pretending to salute Oliver.

They quietly closed the front door and went into the living room. Anne kicked her high heels off and moved her feet around. Oliver went into the kitchen.

'A nightcap for the road?' he said.

'Oh go on then, can you bring me crisps as well?'

He returned, and they sat and chatted about the night.

'I had such a good night, Anne.'

'Ditto, just what the doctor ordered.'

'Do you think Arianna will become closer to Toby? We do need to remember she is his mum,' said Oliver.

'We will be okay, Ollie, she has us to help. We are getting better at letting her do more on her own with Toby. Look at tonight, for example, she never called us once at the club.'

'True, I love you so much, Annie pannie.'

'I love you too, Oliver, soooo much.' They rubbed noses, then Anne said, 'I'm going to go upstairs to put my pyjamas on.'

She got up and left the room. The house was so quiet. On her way upstairs, Anne stopped and looked around. Complete and utter contentment flowed through her veins.

She tiptoed up the stairs. Contentedly anticipating seeing Toby breathing with the rhythmic sound of suck, pause, suck, pause. Imagining his chubby wee cheeks going in and out.

She opened the bedroom door, expecting to see her much-loved grandson, but he was not in his cot. He must be in with Arianna, was her next thought. Curious, she tiptoed to the other room, expecting to see both mum and baby in peaceful slumbers. Instead, Anne found another empty room. With that, the silence was shattered when there was a loud guttural noise and high-pitched screaming.

Oliver jumped and ran into the hall, taking the stairs two at a time. His wife, clearly distressed, pointed towards the rooms. 'Gone, gone, gone!'

'Who?' said Oliver.

'Arianna!'

He looked past his wife who was holding onto the banister to steady herself from the shock. Oliver sprinted towards Toby's room. The cot was empty.

Panic striken, Oliver ran downstairs, picked up the phone and called the police. The police operator listened, 'She is gone, he is gone!' They heard Anne scream in the background and thought this was a domestic violent situation. The call handler was about to go into the professional speech, when the man on the line, said, 'Find them. My baby is gone. So has her baby.'

'Where are you at the moment, sir?

'AT MY HOUSE!' screamed Oliver.

'No, sir, I need your address,' said the calm voice at the other end of the line. 'Sir, you need to calm down.' This attempt at calmness was lost on Oliver who felt like he had been hit by a tsunami.

'I can't!' Oliver screamed. 'Get someone here quick'.

'Who has gone?' the operator again asked.

'My daughter and my grandson!'

'Maybe they have gone to visit a friend.'

'NO they haven't. Get here now, NOW, they were here when we left.'

'Someone will be with you very soon.'

They police did come, but not soon enough for Oliver or Anne. They asked them questions, where had they been, had their daughter planned on going out. 'NO. NO. NO.'

Did she have any money in the house? 'Yes, some savings upstairs for a camera,' replied Oliver.

'Please go and check, also look around to determine if anything else is missing from the baby's room.'

Oliver soon discovered missing clothes from Arianna's room, and some money for the new camera she was saving to buy. The snowsuit put on the baby, every time they went out, plus a couple of babygrows were also gone.

The police call went out for a young mum and her missing infant. The baby was found a few hours later and placed in emergency care after being checked over at the hospital.

Toby never came home to the place he had known since his birth.

Arianna was found a week later living in a bed and breakfast establishment. She had also found work at the local fairground. The police were unable to persuade the young runaway to go home. The double tragedy was that she did not want the baby. She also insisted he was not to be returned to her mum and dad. They were distraught.

It took years for them to stop looking at every infant, then young child, the same age as Toby, as well as young people their daughter's age. They hoped they would eventually see Arianna or their much-loved grandson. The police were eventually able to trace Arianna's calls. They found one particular friend on a social networking site.

The police called round to the house to discuss this with Anne and Oliver. 'Do you know Arianna's friend Belinda?'

'No,' they both said.

'Has she ever spoken about her?' asked the officer.

'No, we are not familiar with that name, officer,' they both said.

'When we did further investigations we found this person was also known as Denise – is that a name Arianna may have mentioned,' asked the other police officer.

They both looked at the policeman, stunned. At the same time both felt the blood drain from their heads, making them feel faint.

The policeman observed this. 'Why don't you both go and sit down? Catch your breath, then tell me what you both know about Denise.'

Chapter Nineteen

Morag was not looking to meet anyone else. One day her door knocked, and she answered the door to the delivery driver.

'I have a parcel for you.' The driver confirmed her name before handing it over.

'Thanks,' said Morag.

'Expecting anything nice?'

'Honestly, I don't know. I do this every year to cheer myself up, order a lot of things from the catalogue for the new season.'

'Very good. See you again then.' The delivery driver laughed.

The chance meeting affected them both. Morag went around all day thinking about the driver. Lovely smile, friendly eyes, she felt an instant attraction, which was unlike her.

The driver, back on daily deliveries, for some reason kept thinking about the woman from number 15. 'Utter tosh,' was said out loud when the presenter said love at first sight was the next bulletin being discussed on the radio.

'I felt an instant attraction and we were married fourteen days later,' said an old woman on the radio. 'We have been married sixty years. He was my soulmate. Went to war and I never knew if I would see him again. After the war we went on to have six wonderful children, grandchildren and now great grandchildren,' said the woman with such affection and love for her husband.

'Aye right, are you serious, hen? You're a minority not the majority. Complete rubbish, only fools believe in love at first sight,' muttered the driver.

Next day, another parcel was to be delivered to number 15, and Glen felt a thrill of anticipation, unsure where it came from.

The door was chapped, then Morag opened the door, and the smile on her face and glint in her eyes was mesmerising.

'You again.'

'Me again. How are you?'

'Good thanks. How are you?'

This went on all week. Both found they were looking forward to seeing the other.

'Did you order the whole catalogue?' The driver laughed.

'You would think so, given the number of deliveries I have had!'

The following week the same pattern emerged, only this time it was returns.

'Not you again,' said the driver. 'This is becoming a habit, I'm beginning to think you want to see me on a daily basis.'

'Oh no, really, I'm not,' said Morag, spluttering with embarrassment.

'I'm joking, don't be so serious. I am enjoying chatting to you, would you believe I'm actually finding myself looking forward to our now daily chats.' The equally embarrassed driver laughed.

'Do you fancy meeting sometime?' said Morag.

'Oh, I'm not sure,' said Glen.

'Never mind. I shouldn't have asked,' said a mortified Morag.

'I've recently come out of a long-term relationship.'

'Me too,' said Morag.

At the end of the following week, Morag handed over the last parcel, and Glen gave her the proof of return.

'Cheers.'

'Last one, been good chatting to you. What's your name?'

'Glen.'

'I am Morag, pleased to have met you.'

'I know,' Glen laughed, pointing to the parcel, 'both your name and address are here.'

'Bye.'

'Bye.'

Morag placed the receipt in the tub beside the fridge. The following week she took it out to check the date of the return. On the other side was Glen's number.

Morag giggled and danced around the kitchen. They must have had a connection.

'Hello.'

'Hello, who is this?'

'Morag from number 15.'

'What took you so long?'

'I put the receipt in the tub last week, and it was purely by chance I took it out today.'

'I was really hoping you would call, you see I couldn't come back round, against company policy, however, because you asked me out, that is different.'

'Believe it or not, that was so bold for me.'

They were on the phone for hours talking about all sorts. Glen talked about the tosh of the bulletin. Morag laughed.

The next day Morag was worried about the boys and what they may say.

'Mark and Michael, I have something to tell you.'

'We will put the washing away, give us time.'

'I want to talk about something else,' said an embarrassed Morag.

'Are you ill, Mum?' said Mark.

'What's wrong?' said Michael.

'I've met someone I would like to go out with. But only if you two are okay with it.'

'MUM, go,' both said in unison.

Although Morag now had the approval of the boys, trepidation set in. Sitting at the table, her mind wandered back to yesteryear and the way things used to be.

Anne was a great help when the boys were young.

'Can you fetch those nappies?'

'YES!'

She also was a great 'wee mum' to them. Anne tried her luck going into the biscuit cupboard when Morag was distracted with the boys, and said, 'Can I have this?' holding up a chocolate biscuit.

'Put it back now, Anne,' Morag would chide. However, on occasions Anne looked at her mum and defiantly took a bite, before running away as fast as a three-year-old could move.

Another time when Mark played on his bike outside, Morag said, 'Do not use your shoes to stop the bike.' Next came a phase of pulling the brakes, to which his mum said, 'You will come a cropper,' only to be met some weeks later with Mark on the doorstep crying and saying, 'I came a cropper.'

***

Morag started dating Glen, and ironically Susan also met someone. Yet it was Anne and Oliver who were miffed. They were worried the women would get hurt. They also felt a strangeness that their mum's were dating again. Till one night, sitting having their evening chat, Oliver said, 'Anne, I feel bad, my mum should be happy. Mum was always there for us. Everyone can see she has a spring in her step. Bouncing here, there and everywhere.'

Oliver tried to mimic a baby lamb. Anne was hysterical at the gangly and awkward antics and. continued to laugh a long time after the joke was over.

'I was thinking the same the other day. They gave us so much time, we need to stop it, Oliver. But what if Glen and Adam come in and start taking over?' Anne sounded scared.

'They won't, Anne, give the mums some credit. Can you believe it, both mums meeting people virtually at the same time?' said Oliver.

***

Returning home one morning, Morag had just spent the night with Glen. Morag hoped to slip in unspotted by the boys. They caught Morag coming into the house trying to be quiet at 6.am the next morning. They crept out from the living room. 'WHAT TIME DO YOU CALL THIS?' both said jovially, pointing at pretend watches.

Morag got such a fright and ran upstairs like a scalded cat, then sat on the bed feeling totally embarrassed. She felt like a teenager who had just been caught by her parents sneaking into the house. Oh no! How does a mother explain this to her sons? Getting undressed, she showered, then slept till eleven. Going back downstairs, no one was around as the boys were in bed, saving her any further embarrassment.

***

Susan did not have to worry about such things. She had lived alone since Anne and Oliver left home. Arianna stayed the odd weekend, either if Anne and Oliver wanted to go out or she fancied a movie night at Gran's.

'Hi, Mum, how are things?' Oliver and Anne had popped in to drop off some requested provisions.

'Is this the right brand?' asked Oliver.

She glanced and said, 'Yes that will do.'

'Are you feeling any better?'

'I'm good, son,' said Susan, who looked more lovesick than unwell to Anne.

'You sure, Susan?' asked her perceptive daughter-in-law.

'I need to speak to you both. Sit down, I will put the kettle on, I need to tell you something. I was waiting on the right moment.'

They both felt worried. Mum must be ill. She must be. No other explanation.

'Do you think she has met someone, Oliver? She looks more lovesick than unwell,' said Anne.

'How would you know?' said Oliver.

'Just a feeling.'

Susan surprised them in the first instance, then the rest of the family, when she announced, 'I met Adam, on the lonely hearts page in the local paper.'

'WHAT?' said Oliver.

'Unless you meet someone at work, then where else can you meet a new friend?' said Susan. 'It was great, actually quite exciting. We phoned back and forward before we met. First time I met him, Jennifer from work came along as my chaperone. She sat in the corner, had a coffee and read,' said a rather buoyant Susan. Now that they both knew.

'You never said anything, Mum,' said a surprised Oliver. 'Who is Jennifer?'

'A girl from the canteen I have known for years, always asks after you, Oliver,' said Susan, now looking quite sheepish.

'I don't know her,' said her now miffed adult son, looking over at Anne who was equally dumbfounded.

'Anyway, it was safer with my chaperone in the corner. There have been other dates, I didn't just jump in, but they turned out to be really creepy,' Susan said to the two shocked faces before her.

Susan saw the stunned look on the young couple's faces, got up and retrieved something from a biscuit tin in the cupboard. Then came back into the living room and handed them the paper with the advert in it.

Contact Adam

Hi, my name is Adam. I have auburn hair with cocoa brown eyes. I am a smart man who says I like working out at the gym. I am truly committed. I sign up and pay my membership every January. Have done for the past five years. This year is different, as my New Year's resolution is that I hope to complete at least one whole year. Up until now, I am ashamed to admit I am probably known as one of the country's statistics, as I believe so many fools do the same thing. Sitting with a belly full of grub between Christmas and New Year, feeling bloated and knowing they need to get fit. I shamefully admit, I am one of the people who starts off with great enthusiasm. My intentions are genuinely good as I always plan to go early morning en route to work. However, by the last week in January, I put the alarm clock on silent, roll over in bed for another five minutes sleep. 'Call me, call me, call me,' says Debbie Harry.

'DID YOU REALLY BELIEVE THAT CRAP, MUM?'

'No, of course, I didn't, I contacted him for a laugh. We then got on very well and I am glad we met.'

'Aw we are so happy for you, Susan, aren't we, Oliver?'

'Mmm.'

'OLIVER!'

'Okay, okay. Yes, Mum, we are pleased. When do we get the privilege of meeting this buffoon?' said her only son. 'I could have come with you rather than, who was it?'

'Jennifer, love.'

'Oliver, how would that have looked? Oh hi, Adam, and there's my son over there giving you the beady eye,' Susan said jovially.

'I'm not pleased, Mum,' said her son pouting.

'What age are you, Oliver?'

'You're my mum.'

***

As soon as the cat was out of the bag, Susan phoned Morag. They giggled and laughed like a couple of teenagers. They also couldn't believe how they had both met people at the same time.

'The universe must have lined up for us,' said Morag, between chuckles.

'Certainly did,' chortled Susan.

'Oh I should let you know you will be getting visitors, they were in here, I asked them to bring in some provisions. Didn't know how else to broach the subject. They are not best pleased with me,' said Susan, laughing again.

'Will keep you posted. Oh, here they come, better go, speak soon.' As they both laughed and hung up the phone.

***

Morag and Glen clicked and were so very happy.

Morag ribbed Glen for ages after that.

'Tell them about your perception of love at first sight.'

'Stop, I was wrong.'

'Come on.'

Pulling out her ear, Glen whispered quietly, 'Tosh.'

'Still of the same opinion over there?' the boys said.

'No,' said Glen, leaning in towards Morag.

Glen was Spanish and a lovely extended family who they all met soon after. The younger generation struggled with the new relationships – actually more Oliver and Anne, watching Glen and Adam cuddle into their mums.

They were often observed, coyly touching their partners' arms. Then sometimes, bashfully, pushing them playfully away. They giggled like teenagers.

'I feel sure we never did that,' said Oliver.

'I find it hard watching them behaving like that, don't you?' said Anne.

'Yes, I find it hard. I want to say, "Leave her alone, that's my mum".'

He quickly realised how childish that would sound coming from a grown man with a family.

The relationships developed, then Morag and Glen decided to make it official. They were one of the first same-sex couples to marry, making it official just after midnight on the 21st January 2015. They had a wonderful day and do 'live happily ever after' with their families.

'I'm so happy I ordered all those clothes,' Morag said not long after they married.

'I cannot believe how happy and content I feel,' said Glen.

Dave was disgusted when he found out. He came round to tell them in no uncertain terms. Glen said, 'Get lost, Dave,' kissed Morag, then shut the door on his aghast face, before creasing with laughter behind the door.

They heard him shout, 'You are disgusting, Morag, and if the children were younger, they would be coming to live with me.' Morag started to cry, then Glen said, 'Don't let a narrow-minded twat like him get to you.'

'I won't.'

Chapter Twenty

The years passed, Oliver and Anne's life took a significantly different turn from what they had hoped. They still struggled to accept it was Arianna's choice to leave.

One night while Anne made supper, Oliver's' phone pinged. Oliver clicked on Facebook. His friend Robert from Portsmouth had posted photographs. They'd met many years before when Robert had been up to visit family. They got on so well that they became friends from afar, becoming pen pals. They chatted back and forward over the years, about this and that. They both loved the same football team. They never really discussed Arianna leaving, so Robert always assumed they had no children. Because they seemed to have so much in common, they'd recently discussed meeting up but life seemed to get in the way. They haven't managed to catch up yet, always meaning to, definitely next year.

Oliver looked more closely at the photographs, then felt the colour drain from his face when he realised he recognised someone in the background of one of the photographs. He shouted, 'ANNE, COME HERE QUICK!'

'Oh, Oliver, stop being so dramatic,' said Anne who had just plated his favourite supper, roasted cheese and tomato.

'NO, ANNE, really, you need to come,' he shouted louder.

She thought he had taken unwell and felt her legs shake before rushing through.

'Look!'

'Honestly, Oliver, you are so dramatic. What am I looking at?'

Anne sat on the edge of the settee, looking over at the photograph on Oliver's phone, her legs and head even weaker. 'That's ... that's ... our Arianna. Contact him now! Find out why she is there!'

Oliver private messaged his friend, playing the whole thing down. 'Hi, mate, looks like a great night.'

Ping. 'Yes, going really well. Hope you and Anne are well. We will definitely catch up soon, coming up to see family in a few weeks.'

'We are well, thanks. That's a plan, mate. Was wondering if you know the people in the last photograph?'

'Will let you know. Bye for now.'

The following week Robert got back to them and said it was a work colleague or acquaintance of his wife. She vaguely knew the guy, works with him, a new start. She invited them to the party because she thought it would help them settle into the area, being new and not really having got to know anyone. The invite was also extended to give them a chance to meet the friendship groups already established. 'Trish thought it would be good for them to come along to meet everyone.'

'Can you possibly pass on my details, mate? I think I may know them, lost touch years ago.'

'No problem, leave it with me, will be in touch soon as I hear anything,' said Robert.

An assurance was given that Trish would speak with the guy in the photograph on Monday when they returned to work.

They waited and waited. Nothing happened. Week after week passed, and the checking became obsessive.

'Has she found out anything yet?' said Anne.

'We can't push this, Anne.'

'Has she?' said Anne impatiently.

'Don't know. We need to be patient, hard as it is.'

There were tears night after night until Oliver said, 'Enough, Anne, we can't go back there. We have to move on.'

'You're right, Oliver, it's just so hard. It's like the cut has been opened in my heart and it physically hurts.'

'I know. I feel the same. We have done our best, Anne,' said her equally sad husband.

'I know we have.'

They had a plan, which they established years ago, every so often when they relapsed, this pattern helped them cope with the grief. After five years, their way of moving on. If they felt sad and missed Arianna, they both agreed to light a candle.

'We hope you are shining bright wherever you are, Arianna,' they would both say, then cried for their lost family. This has been done so many times over the years.

They would also recite, 'If you love something let it go. If it's yours it will come back to you. If it doesn't, it never was.' Even as they said this, it was heartbreaking, trying to accept she did not want to be in touch with her family.

After carrying out their ritual, two days later a private message from Robert appeared for Oliver on Facebook. They were beside themselves.

'The guy was a bit vague, asked if I can I pass on your address?'

'Yes, mate, that would be great.'

Over the next few years it was very slow, as Arianna did not want to speak to Mum only Dad. She felt her mum let her down more than her dad. They had to accept this or lose all contact again. There was sporadic contact and never by social media, having never used it again after the terrible experience which changed her life forever.

She never believed her dad would really have kissed Denise. Mum on the other hand had been pregnant with her and taken prescription drugs. Did she not know that at 16–19 weeks when an unborn baby ingests the sweet amniotic fluid it takes in larger quantities than if the fluid were bitter?

Arianna had done a lot of research about nature or nurture. Initially wondering if this was the reason her life choices had had this devastating impact.

Understandably, Anne and Oliver had initially hoped for more contact.

'Listen, I think you both need to give her time,' said Susan.

'I am so delighted we know she is safe,' said a tearful Morag. 'Life works in mysterious ways. At least we know she is safe, let's go and light a candle, maybe she will come around.'

***

'What did I do wrong?' Anne cried in her husband's arms the next day after telling their parents about Arianna.

'Don't know, Anne,' said her husband, equally heartbroken for his wife.

This has been the pattern for years. Anne and Oliver were getting ready to celebrate another anniversary. Few believed they would have survived those first few years. The gossip was awful. 'We give them two years at the most, then one of them will be off to seek his or her fortune. You must remember his dad up and left when he was a baby, and her mum married a woman,' Anne overheard a couple of gossips say at the checkout queue, unaware she was behind them.

The party was planned and they were heading to a local club in a few hours. Arianna had said she would attend.

As they were getting toshed up for the evening, Oliver began to hyperventilate. 'Anne, I don't know if I can do this. Look, I am shaking.'

'I am too, Oliver. I think I am going to be sick.'

Anne regained composure first, then said, 'Oliver, we have waited this long.'

'Do you really think she will come?' said Oliver.

'I really hope so.'

Chapter Twenty-One

They were enjoying the party with their family and friends while frequently looking at the door. Then their favourite song 'Don't Look Back in Anger' by Oasis was played, and they both got up and started dancing.

They were waiting for Arianna Scott, wife and mother to twin girls and a boy; it was her husband who supported his wife to make the trip to the party.

'Do you want me to come with you, Arianna?'

'No. I really want to try to go on my own. As I left on my own, I want to return on my own. Do you understand what I mean?'

'I do understand, although I don't want you to be frightened on your own, Arianna.'

'Pinky promise, I will tell you.'

'Pinky promise, I believe you.' Her husband smiled.

After kissing the family goodbye, en route to the railway station, they chatter away.

'Do you think I am doing the right thing?' asked Arianna. 'Some wounds are better left closed, don't you think?'

'I think it's the right thing as long as you're okay, Arianna.'

Gathering her luggage together, her husband stood at the side of the car. 'Bye, good luck'

'Bye. Don't forget the girls go to Brownies tomorrow and the football training for—'

Before she could mention their son, her husband replied, 'Go or you will miss the train. We will cope to a fashion.'

'That's what I am frightened of,' said his wife who kissed and cuddled him before departure.

The sound of the train was mesmerising, and she began to feel trepidation slip in. So much so that when the train stopped for the connecting train she went for a coffee and pondered what to do. This resulted in the return journey home happening on the same day as the departure.

Her husband was waiting. Arianna ran to his arms and sobbed for some time. The trip had been a step too far.

She really did try, however, in the end never arrived at the anniversary party.

***

After the party Oliver and Anne regretfully shared their thoughts.

'I am so sad she never made it.'

'I am too.'

'Do you think we were hoping for our little girl back?' said a forlorn Oliver.

'I was thinking that too. Maybe, Oliver, as my heart was skipping similar to when she was a little girl. Remember when she won that race at nursery and came running over to us and shouted, "Look I woned it," and you scooped her up and said, "You won the race, Arianna, well done, you ran faster than the wind." "Me did," she said, proud as punch.' Anne laughed at the memory.

'I know. Now we can never be the parents to Arianna we would love to have been,' said Oliver.

'We will never be close to our grandchildren,' said Anne. 'We must accept that, Oliver. Our lives were changed forever. Arianna may never forgive me for not telling her about the painkillers when I was pregnant with her. I hope that the ebb and flow of the chromosome trick never catches Arianna's children as it did their gran,' Anne said, full of sadness. 'Lying dormant, then triggered by the environment. I did take prescription drugs at that low ebb during my teenage years. I wish, I wish, I wish,' said a tearful Anne.

'Shh, love, don't do that to yourself. Let's wait and see if she gets in touch. Maybe she just got scared. She has been away for so long,' said her dad.

***

It took Arianna years to trust anyone after leaving home.

'Why did I do it?' she asked the GP over and over again, who then referred her for counselling.

At the top of the stairs there was an arrow and a name on the door. When Arianna opened it, she instantly felt the welcoming ethos. Once inside the room the friendly receptionist took her name and asked her to sit down. 'Maureen will be with you shortly, she is running a bit late.' Once seated her eyes and ears were stimulated. The room was furnished in pastel colours and soothing music played in the background. The fish tank in the corner was strategically placed, where the tranquil flow of water balanced the sounds coming through the speakers. The pictures on the walls were of green trees and sunsets.

'Arianna,' said the friendly voice.

'Yes,' said Arianna, jumping to attention, more through fear of her emotions than the friendly face in front of her.

'Pleased to meet you. I am Maureen. How are you today?'

'Mmm,' muttered a subdued Arianna.

'Please follow me, Arianna.' Maureen opened the door to reveal a room that was a replica of the waiting room. 'Please take a seat and make yourself comfortable.'

'Thanks,' Arianna said, then unconsciously sat on her feet, before pushing her whole body sideways in the chair almost like the foetal position.

'This is a safe place, Arianna, whatever we talk about in here stays in here, except should I think you are at risk. Whereby I am duty bound to protect lives and must report it,' said Maureen as she went through the confidentiality agreement, which would be signed by both. 'This can help clients to feel secure, knowing what they share is confidential, Arianna.'

'It was my fault.'

'Arianna, why do you think that?' said the counsellor. 'I have already read the notes from the GP.'

'Why did I turn into a monster? What made me that person? Rebelling, angry, unhappy, and able to give my baby away and move on?'

'Why do you think you did that?'

'Because I clicked a button and was groomed by an adult.'

'Exactly, you were a child.'

'Why didn't I talk to Mum or Dad? We were so close.'

'Why do you think?'

'Because I was manipulated and set up by that bitch.'

'What bitch?'

'Belinda who lied to me to get even with my mum and dad.'

'You did not initiate that, Arianna, please remember that. You were the unfortunate victim of a vindictive individual.'

'But I walked away from my baby, and I am happy never to see him again.'

'Why did you walk away?'

'I was suffocating in the trap that Belinda wove. I was enticed into her web of deceit. "Come into my web," said the spider to the fly.'

Arianna went for further counselling again before getting married and having children.

'What if the first pregnancy left scars so deep that I fear I may do it again. What if I don't bond with another baby? Would I give them away as easily as Toby? Maureen, what do you think?'

'What was it about Toby?'

'I never wanted him. I don't even know who his dad was, I was drunk. I was encouraged by Belinda. I didn't like him, even when I pretended he was my wee brother.'

'You were in conflict, Arianna, understandably so. Do you think you are the same person?'

'NO.'

'Then why do you think you would do this again?'

'Don't know.'

The following week, sitting in the waiting room, Arianna read an article on early stages of development.

Did you know? That the amniotic fluid constantly moves (circulates) as the baby swallows and inhales the fluid, then releases it.

Arianna thought, *Is it possible that, as it ebbs and flows, this golden liquid can also trick the chromosomes into mutating, stay dormant, then be stimulated negatively at a later date? After all, mum was addicted to prescription drugs in the early stages of pregnancy with me – Is it possible the amniotic fluid ingested by all babies can, in fact, change their path in history?*

Getting angry at the simplicity of the article, she muttered louder than expected, 'Why else would a loving daughter have gone completely off the rails, so easily, or been influenced by someone so horrible?'

'Are you okay over there?' said the receptionist.

'Yes, sorry, was looking for something, didn't realise you could hear me.'

'Hi, Arianna, sorry I am running late.'

'No problem, Maureen.'

Going into the room, Maureen said, 'Are you okay, Arianna? You look a bit flustered.'

'That article is a load of rubbish out there.' She pointed to the door as if the counsellor knew what she was talking about.

'What article?'

'In that magazine out there, it talked about amniotic fluid, saying the baby ingests it. Made me feel really angry about my mum and her stuff,' said a very agitated Arianna.

'Do you want to talk about it?'

'That bitch knew at the time what she was doing to me. Social media is an unmanned evil monster. Did you know she pretended to be the same age as me? Callously encouraged me to drink, sleep with boys … Can you imagine what it was like that night when I needed Belinda most? She left me alone and I left the baby in the hospital. Was that whole debacle my fault? I still torture myself.'

Maureen handed her the box of hankies when she noticed the silent tears rolling down her cheeks. Arianna took one and wiped the tears away.

'Arianna, you were used as a weapon against both your parents. A vulnerable teenager who trusted someone, believing they were a friend, who turned out to be nothing more than a vindictive individual. Who then displayed negative premeditated actions which changed the path of so many lives.'

'You're right, Maureen. I really thought I was sorted. I can't understand where that anger came from just reading an article.'

'Where do you think it came from? You could try writing down your thoughts before we meet again.'

'Mmm,' said Arianna.

'You lost everything in this whole situation. I can see from your records you have resolved so much conflict, Arianna' said Maureen trying to offer some reassurance.

The notes in her file started several years before.

> *January – During the tortured years, Arianna wondered many times why in that moment of distress she never called her mum and dad when Belinda AKA Denise had blocked all calls. Arianna is very distressed.*
>
> *Arianna was referred here by the GP. This homeless young woman is trying to resolve internal conflict. Today's session allowed the distressed Arianna the opportunity to discuss and deal with the guilt. The loss of Toby with no desire to reconnect was also discussed.*
>
> <u>*MA 10th January*</u>
>
> *February – Another issue raised today was that Arianna's Mum and Dad were having a night out. Arianna appears to carry emotional baggage. As a result, this appears to trigger feelings of all-consuming self-reproach of having spoiled their lives. Guilt she had Toby in the first place. In foolishly being influenced negatively*

*by Belinda, who told her to go with a couple of boys.
Then not knowing who the baby's dad was appals her.
Coming from a loving family the guilt being felt by
Arianna is all consuming, with terrible feelings of shame
having been discussed.*

<u>*MA 18th February*</u>

*March – Arianna was compromised. Being considered a
miss goody two shoes, was forced to fit into the
expectations of her new BFF.*

<u>*MA 12th March*</u>

*April – Arianna talked freely about the negative feelings
around being forced to push boundaries. This did not
bode well for Arianna as she complied with the peer
pressure and carried out these terrible acts. With each act
of defiance, Arianna continues to feel she betrayed her
loving parents. This has set up a conflict and perceived
fear, having breached moral codes instilled by her
family.*

<u>*MA 27th April*</u>

*May – Arianna knew something wasn't right as this new
friend quizzed her about her dad and a kiss. Unable to
solve this, ultimately, the decision to lie to her parents
did not come naturally to the youngster. It would appear
she acted as she did to avert the wrath of her new best
friend. This friend also appears to have feigned an
understanding of life as a teenager. The pull to fit in
became stronger than the will to admit defeat to her
friend. Arianna did not wish to betray this very special
friend. Living in their family meant this particular
teenager knew nothing about parties, drink, being*

accepted by peers and lots of other things which Belinda knew.

MA 27th May

June – Arianna has shared that once the awful truth emerged it became clear it was not a peer. It was in fact an adult grooming a child in order to abuse and manipulate them. Did her dad really kiss that pretend girl's mum? Was it Denise (not her alias Belinda) who kissed him? Arianna is finding it hard to comprehend what made Belinda so vindictive and evil. Through further discussions, Arianna has concluded that Belinda was an extremely dangerous and bad person. She also asked was Belinda's behaviour towards her a catalyst to trigger her body's extreme response to seek comfort through addiction?

MA 18th June

July – Arianna is asking is it also possible that this human lottery could account for how Belinda's cells may have mutated and twisted? After she ingested the amniotic fluid while in her mother's womb? Did it then mutate very negatively to produce Belinda, who then shared with Arianna that, as child as young as four, she enjoyed power and control over other much younger children. While playing schools she shared that she had to be the teacher. Put a drawing pin on a child seat, knowing it would inflict pain, then sneered when the child cried.

MA 15th July

August – Arianna arrived very withdrawn. In the session she shared, due to her actions the night she abandoned her baby, she feels consumed with dread and fear. She is agitated and couldn't sit still in tonight's session. She talked a lot about how she narrowly escaped a custodial sentence. She was told by the police they would have charged her with child abandonment had she left Toby in the bag of rolls that night. By being left behind in a public place, it meant the baby would quickly be found when he cried for food or comfort very soon after Arianna left. While being interviewed, Arianna innocently shared with the police the first thought of leaving baby instead outside a local pub in a bag of rolls. Arianna said the policewoman sensitively informed her had she done that it would have been classed as a very different crime, under child abandonment laws.

Arianna is being encouraged to work on forgiving herself by trying not to focus on what could have been rather than what did happen.

<u>MA 21st August</u>

September – Arianna believes both her mum and dad would have helped had they known the predicament their daughter was in. Recalling her actions and behaviours, she is very distressed and cried in today's session. Arianna said she is unable to process what actually happened that night. She continues to wonder what she did that was so bad to make Belinda decide to remove her as a FRIEND.

Arianna has processed and is saying she is relieved a custodial sentence was avoided due to the circumstances surrounding the case. She feels relieved it was eventually dismissed, once background searches were done. Arianna does not carry any guilt, and feels she did the right thing leaving Toby. She also shared that once the police found Toby, he was put up for long-term fostering with a view to adoption. Arianna feels this allowed her to be free of the baby, who for her was put up with rather than loved. The safe haven law was used as protection from a jail sentence. The fact Toby was well looked after, meeting all his milestones, went favourably for the teenage mum. The fact he was dropped off in the local hospital toilets also was in her favour.

MA 5th September

Chapter Twenty-Two

The family nor Arianna never found out what happened to Toby before the adoption papers were signed. The infant went into long-term foster care due to the mum being willing to let this baby go forever.

One night Morag and Susan were on the telephone. Both remained heartbroken at the loss of their beloved granddaughter and great-grandson.

'How are you?' asked Susan.

'Not good at all. You?'

'Same, I can't stop crying. I'm off work at the moment, I can't think properly.'

'Arianna was such a good girl, we would have helped with Toby,' said an equally devasted Morag. 'I used to say to her when she was little, it's like having your mum back as a little girl when you come to visit Arianna. Such a delight and a pleasure, you make your gran so happy. Why didn't our girl come to me and tell me what was happening?'

'I don't know, Morag, that's what is upsetting me the most,' said Susan.

'Social media has a lot to answer for. Why are such travesties still happening? Did you see in the papers there is even a bullying campaign in November to raise awareness and address the issues of online bullying and grooming?'

'A little too late for our family,' said a very sad Susan.

'I can still feel embarrassed, Susan, why didn't we know?'

'So can I. I met Mrs Dempster in the Co-op, she was telling me five young people had hung themselves within the local area and asked had I heard about it. I did see that in the local paper last week,' said Susan.

Chapter Twenty-Three

Morag is standing at the sink washing the dishes, distracted by her thoughts, watching the cars pass by at the top of the road, taking people here and there and everywhere. *What are their stories,* she wonders, totally exhausted from another day sitting in court listening to a lawyer defend an unforgivable act.

'Case 2542.'

Once sworn in the lawyer started by saying, 'Your honour, my client is extremely sorry for this situation.'

Reflecting back, Morag muttered to herself, 'We as a family are not just another case number in court with an inept lawyer who can't possibly believe this is a good case. Defending the unforgivable, how can this be justice?'

Glen comes up behind her and says, 'Talking to yourself again, darling?'

'I didn't hear you come in. I was saying, we as a family are not just another case number in that court with a lawyer who can't possibly believe this is a good case to be defending. Yet is paid to do a job. How is this called justice, Glen?'

'I don't think it is.'

'That whatsherface bad bitch who devastated our Arianna's life through sheer badness.' The anger starts to rise within Morag.

'There is nothing I can add, we need to wait, Morag.'

'You're right, I am just so angry. A: looking at her pathetic face and B: the unnecessary devastation to our family,' said Morag.

'Let's get tidied up, watch a bit of TV, then bed, as you have to get up and go again tomorrow,' said Glen, sympathetically.

'It's so hard to listen to the evidence. Our whole family and Susan's have been questioned about why our Arianna disappeared without any warning. It was so difficult, with all the stories in the press. Implied we were not as it first appeared. A strong family who supported Anne and Oliver, young parents who now face their daughter being classed as a runaway.'

The pain of the court case had unsettled Morag and Susan. Both hoped, as they listened to this trial, it would give them some closure against the vindictive woman who wrecked their lives, and the lives of their immediate and extended family.

'Surely she can't walk free, Morag?' said Susan, leaving the court equally exhausted.

Both had been crying throughout the day thinking about Arianna and Toby. It was extremely difficult to sit and listen to the evidence being presented by the defence. They both wanted to shout, 'You cannot be serious!'

The heading in the paper was shattering: *Runaway teenager Versus grooming teacher, who do you believe?'*

The rest of the family did nothing to warrant the uninvited attention and public comments directed at them in the paper. The ongoing implications were that there must have been something hidden in their family life the public were unaware of. Why else would Arianna behave in such a way, leaving her baby at the local hospital?

Susan and Morag hurried past the reporters.

Susan huddled in close to Morag and said, '"Tut tut," I used to hear when Oliver was a baby. "Single mum with no morals," they would try to whisper as I passed, then rub the side of their noses. I knew what they were saying. Even when I used to go round to my friends and cry, she would say, "Seven day wonder, Susan, today's news for them, is tomorrow's chip wrapping paper for us. Don't let them get to you." Jennifer from work was so good, she would get up, give me a cuddle and say, "Onwards and upwards."'

Susan had a long hot bath to try to ease the tension in her body from sitting in court all day. She poured a glass of red wine, then curled up on the couch. Unable to settle or calm her inner thoughts, like tumbleweed they gathered momentum.

'We were a family who stuck together through thick and thin. Why was this allowed to happen in a civilised society? Oh my God, I sound like my mum! Social media should be banned forever from youngsters Arianna's age; it's the curse of the everyday person now.'

Susan also remembers having a conversation with one of the managers from another department before the all-staff meeting.

'Phones they are the bain of my life,' said Tom.

'I feel quite lucky, Tom, as most people in the office I manage don't use their phones unless it's their breaks. I have heard other managers, like you say, have lost count of how many times they have to say, "Put your phones away, you are at work."'

'They don't seem to realise they aren't being paid to be posting on social media. That it could result in disciplinary or even worse losing their jobs!'

The next day, once sworn in, the lawyer for the prosecution said, 'All I know is one click of a button negatively changed the course of this family's life forever. Bullies thrive on power, and what better platform than a medium as far reaching as the one they lost their daughter, Arianna, to? How do the victims of bullying, like Arianna, get help? Can it be attributed to the increase in suicide of some vulnerable young people? Would the things said on social media by young people be said face to face or verbalised in a telephone conversation? No? So, my question is why is this acceptable behaviour on a public forum, from an adult pretending to be a child? The psychology behind this is very sinister, when an adult can groom a child and the child is unaware. These algorithms, the trails they create, are they the problem?

'Exhibit five is now being shown to the court,' said the lawyer. 'A click of a button and a young woman befriended this adult. I ask, Your Honour, are mobile phones progress or the demise of society given what happened to this family? Arianna would never have encountered Denise, and if she had, would Denise have asked for her phone number, then started harassing her, highly unlikely. Yet she was able to create a false profile and manipulate Arianna at the most vulnerable stage in her young adolescent life.'

'Mmm, I would like to adjourn until tomorrow,' said the judge. 'All stand.'

That night, Susan had another glass of wine, this time with some nibbles. Adam arrived home after a late meeting.

'How did it go today?'

She burst into tears. 'One of the hardest things I have ever had to do, Adam, is sit and listen to that woman's lawyer try and defend her by suggesting middle child syndrome and the impact of that on her self-esteem.'

'Shsh.' He hugged her. 'It will be hard, Susan, you know my thoughts on the woman. The scum of society, physical, mental and emotional abusers should be locked up and the keys thrown away. Predators like her are so deviant, while pretending to be something else. Come into my web says the spider to the fly. I know what I would do with her.'

'Adam, there is no point. I know one day she will get her comeuppance if karma has its way.'

'Are you okay now, Susan?'

'No, I have to do it all again tomorrow, go and listen to the lawyer put forward pathetic excuses for why she behaved as she did to our Arianna.'

'I'm glad I can come tomorrow.'

'So am I,' said Susan, moving closer to feel the comfort from Adam's body.

***

The next day, the whole family left broken hearted. Anne and Oliver never got over it and were forced to create a different life from what they had imagined. Regrets of not inviting Arianna to live with them can still hurt her loving grandparents.

'We all saw that wonderful girl struggle,' said Morag to Glen, leaving court. 'The whole family thought it was teenage angst.'

Susan said to Adam as they were leaving the court, 'So many times over the years Oliver came and just sat at the table. Seeing the pain etched on his face distressed me so much. He was riddled with guilt for years, and there was nothing I could do.

"You did nothing wrong, Oliver," I constantly told him, "that woman did."'

They sat together on so many nights, heartbroken, and chatted into the wee small hours. They were all becoming obsessive until after many years they had to let it go. Try to build a different life without Arianna or baby Toby. There was nothing any of them could do. This was a young adult who had choices, which had to be respected.

'I hear what you are saying, Susan, I don't know what to say.'

'There is nothing you can say, Adam.'

'I know,' said Adam. Back at the car, the radio blared as soon as Adam started the engine. This broke the moment. Then Susan burst into tears again.

***

Another day dawned, the family were in court watching intently, waiting on the woman who destroyed their families get her just desserts. None of them were vindictive people. They were all realists. The woman they saw in the dock was a contradiction in terms. Denise appeared well spoken. Dressed in clothes from Oliver Bonas, she appeared to engage with the lawyer with nods and smiles.

'All rise, court adjourned for lunch.'

Susan and Morag ate lunch together as Anne and Oliver had gone on an errand. Susan said, 'That woman is so disingenuous, trying to play the judge with her lawyer allowing this to happen. Why?'

'Oh, Susan, I'm sure the judge knows exactly what is happening,' said Morag.

'Both lawyers have years of experience,' said Susan.

'How do you know that?' said Morag.

'I googled both firms the lawyers work for. I charted their individual careers, they're both very capable.'

'Why did you do that?' asked Morag.

'In the hope that ours will see through that fake person who deliberately destroyed everything we held precious. Can you believe that someone would wait all those years, hang onto such bitterness, then become so twisted? I hope they throw the book at her. Did you ever see that one coming?'

'No. Never.'

'Me neither. She well and truly whipped the rug from under us all,' said Susan.

They had both felt the gap in the family, and the loss of Arianna so deeply. In some ways a small part of their hearts had died. There were no answers. There were many sleepless nights. There was pain and anger. Morag and Susan were stunned. They all survived the early days with Anne and Oliver, to then have to deal with this. They were ill equipped given the magnitude of the situation. They all rallied together and supported each other. However, one question always lay unanswered.

WHY?

Chapter Twenty-Four

I s it possible that when Denise ingested the sweet amniotic fluid, that it distorted and twisted her genetic makeup , creating this bad person?

'A master manipulator,' the judge said, 'she often used tears to defend off any unwanted challenges, which may just expose who she truly was. This power-driven individual, when questioned in the police station, claimed to have low self-esteem. Claimed environmental influences negatively affected her, as the middle child in her family. And you, her lawyer, tried to justify this as a reasonable excuse?'

'I am sorry, your honour,' said the now-shamed lawyer.

'Irrespective of the current research around middle child syndrome, I do not accept this as a reasonable explanation for the vile behaviour I have heard being defended here in my courtroom. Do you hear me?'

'Yes, your honour,' said the lawyer, lowering his head.

The trial had to go to the high court to ensure Denise's sentence was severe enough. 'This will stop and deter anyone else from trying a similar crime.' Before sentencing, the judge said,

'I reiterate, I am appalled at the vain attempt of this deviant character, and her futile attempt to cry her way out of taking responsibility. Your cruel actions, grooming a child for your own gratification, is truly deplorable. These crocodile tears are a little too late. If truly repentant, you would have stopped such evil actions against a child. Do you have anything to say?'

'No, your honour,' replied the now very subdued Denise.

'You were in a position of power as a head teacher. Part of your job is being entrusted with the safety and ongoing support of every young life you meet. Not destroy them through bullying. It has become crystal clear to me that clearly the immature vendetta against the victim's parents, while appalling, was your motive and this lasted many years.

'Do you have anything to say?' the judge added.

'No, your honour.'

'Charges also brought against you include an abuse of power by using school equipment, to access and use students' private information to satisfy your own ends. Further proving you are not the trustworthy individual you led the local authority to believe.'

In the final conclusion, the judge said, before passing the maximum custodial sentence, 'Denise needs to be kept in a secure unit for safety reasons. My job is to protect the public from one less individual like you who can prey on young children while pretending to be their friends. There is no room in society for deviant behaviour such as this. The prison sentence given here today, should allow plenty of time to reflect on the impact bullying has on the lifespan of any individual, regardless of age. Human rights indeed, clearly for you, only go one way. Take the prisoner down to the cells.'

***

Denise was incarcerated and placed in a new environment. Round the clock observations were required for the first few days, from behind the screen, in an effort to try to familiarise her with her long jail sentence.

Almost like a primate on view, scientists, if experimenting, may discuss if it was nature or nurture. Denise, now animated, held her hands up as if addressing a large audience, and smiled in a sly, cunning way.

'Anne, Anne. Call me. Call me. Call me,' she sang like Debbie Harry, then bowed before saying, 'I still haven't heard from you. Smug little bitch, always been a thorn in my side for as long as I can remember. "I love my job." I hated that about you, especially being only a nursery nurse, not like me. Your SUPERIOR, SUPERIOR a head teacher, HEAD TEACHER, ANNE, DO YOU HEAR THAT?' Silence, then the twitching started, closing one eye and blinking rapidly.

This reminded the guard of the inspector in the Peter Seller movies so very long ago. 'Are you okay in there?'

'WHAT?' said Denise, jumping and looking around to detect where the voice came from. 'GO AWAY! DO YOU KNOW WHO I AM? THE HEAD TEACHER OF THAT NEW PRIMARY UP THE ROAD!'

'Not anymore, love,' said the guard, and another laughed in the background. 'You are now here at Her Majesty's pleasure, till further notice.'

'SHUT UP!' Denise shouted. Then going to the corner, she crouched down before sitting down and rocking back and forward. Without warning, she rose, running towards the door, clearly experiencing a flight or fight reaction. Almost like a wild animal trapped in a contained space. Denise hit the wall with such force that she fell back and was dead by the time her body reached the floor. The CPS reported that prisoner XY Denise Brown died early February. There were no suspicious circumstances.

The national news reported it, along with the local newspaper: *'How the mighty have fallen.'*

However, it wasn't until later in the week that more people became aware who the article was about. They had called her Brown by mistake. The next week, the paper entered an apology for any distress to the family, adding the correct surname. Being well known, this provoked many discussions in the community. Not for the reasons Denise craved to be remembered. The newspapers covered the story again. Along with citing a desire to have policies upgraded by the local authority. Some of the parents petitioned the local authority, enquiring how that appointment of head teacher had ever been made in the first place.

> *'Arrogant to the end, without realising that what you put out in the world will always come back to you, but never how you predict. Unearned confidence of that, about which one is ignorant, often has the brightest glow. Denise's glow went out that day. It can only be hoped that while her ashes are dispersed out into the atmosphere, the energy created will move the world forward a little further, to a place where bullying is not used as an excuse towards the nature nurture debate. That it is arrested, once and for all, and no longer like a cancerous condition, seeping and permeating into the very fabric of society. For bullies like Denise, is it pre or post birth, will we ever know?' Dom.frees@newsbynews. com*

The next week Dom felt compelled to include this email from one of his loyal readers:

> *'How many more Ariannas must we read about before something is done? Your article in last week's paper both interested and saddened me. What about the serious, irrevocable ramifications for Oliver, Anne and Arianna and their extended families? It's unforgiveable that such a serious issue continues with no accountability. Except when the person slips up, only then was this monster held to account, when it falls into a criminal act. Why? I agree, Dom, the question still remains: are bullies like Denise born or created? Is it nature or nurture, will we ever know?'*

Chapter Twenty-Five

Having never arrived at the anniversary party, Arianna anticipated her parents disappointment and contacted her dad by letter to apologise.

Hi Dad,
Sorry, I never made it to the party last week. I did try to come. It was too hard.
Best wishes,
Arianna

The deep regret stayed for months.

'I do want to see them, Gareth, I just don't know how to do it.'

'What do you think if we went to the Lake District and we could meet up on neutral territory?'

'That's a good idea. It will provide an ideal opportunity to meet them for a short time. Let me make an excuse and leave if it's too much.'

As a result, it was arranged Anne and Oliver would come to meet Mrs Arianna Scott, her husband, Gareth, and their children. It was stilted to begin with, from afar they could be perceived as strangers who were forced to share a table due to limited space.

Since that first meeting, they continued to get together in the restaurant overlooking Lake Windermere. Bittersweet memories on beautiful days were made. Each time it felt better than the time before.

They met the following month. Arianna was becoming more comfortable, leaning forward to hug both her mum and dad. At the end of this visit, before parting, Arianna suggested coming to visit in her family's home town.

'Would you like to come and visit us next time?' said Arianna.

'Oh my, Arianna, nothing would give us more pleasure,' said Oliver.

'Not to stay though, if that's okay.'

'Of course, love, we will book a hotel.'

Anne couldn't speak as the flow of tears started, rolling down her cheeks. She turned quickly away so the children did not see. Back in the car before setting off on the return journey home, she let out a loud shout, 'Whoopee!'

Oliver reciprocated by also shouting, 'Whoopee!' then pretended to punch Anne's hand.

'Oh, Oliver,' said Anne, bursting into tears again, 'I hope it's okay.'

'Arianna made the first move, it will be.'

Anne and Oliver were both delighted and frightened.

***

The next month they were both quiet in the car on the drive down. Deep in their thoughts, both frightened that, if they messed up, they would lose Arianna again. Both remembering back to when the contact was first established. They'd been ecstatic when Arianna suggested after the first meeting that they put a date in the diary. Try to meet on a more regular basis. The children asked when they would meet Anne and Oliver again last month before they left.

The silence was broken when Anne said, 'It feels strange our grandchildren calling us Anne and Oliver, don't you think?'

'I suppose it does. It made me sad that they really have no bond with us, we are like strangers to them, did you feel it too, Anne?'

'I did and I didn't want to upset you.'

'Aw, Anne, we need to talk about this, not ignore it, we will just have to take it slowly and let Arianna be the one to now move this forward.'

'Agreed,' Anne said, handing Oliver a treacle toffee.

'Is that all you have? Can I have a mint instead?'

'Yes, you can, Oliver,' she said with much affection.

The visit went well. They enjoyed the luxury of the hotel they had chosen.

'Will we make it a bit of a holiday?' asked Anne, as their mums had given them money towards the stay.

'Treat yourselves on us,' Morag and Susan said after handing them a good luck card with money in it.

'We can't accept this.'

'Oh, you can,' they both said in unison. 'We are so happy for you both. Take it and treat yourselves to a meal or an extra night away.'

They booked the lakeside hotel and spa, a traditional hotel with beautiful outlooks.

That day, the family met up and Arianna seemed a bit nervous, before saying, 'I do hope you did not think me rude asking you to stay in a hotel.'

'We understand, Arianna, we would never push you to do anything you're not comfortable doing,' said Anne.

'I know you wouldn't.'

Anne felt the emotion rise before making eye contact with Arianna who gave a wry smile, then looked at her husband Gareth who put his arm around Arianna.

'I told you they would understand,' he said, pulling his wife closely into him. She felt and welcomed the warmth of that emotional contact. It let the fear that was threatening to overtake her dissipate.

'Can you come here, Oliver?' shouted his grandson.

'That's not fair, I wanted him to come with me,' said his granddaughter.

'I think I will be able to go with you all, we have plenty of time.'

'Oliver, Granddad, me first.' The youngest was instructed by her brothers, 'You go with Anne, Gran.'

Arianna's path had been unnecessarily difficult. From afar, if you judged the people meeting outside this hotel, they could be middle-class couples from a quaint part of the country. If judging even further, a wonderful couple with three beautiful children. Born with a silver spoon in their mouths and doting grandparents, here for a visit, choosing to stay in a four-star hotel.

Arianna came over one of the nights after dinner to spend time with her parents, and they sat by the open fire and chatted for hours.

'I missed you both so much. Once I left him, I thought you would hate me, I let you both down.'

'You never let us down, Arianna,' they both said in unison. 'You were betrayed and groomed by a vindictive individual.'

'I still have no regrets about giving away the baby, which made me feel like a monster for many years. What mother has no regrets about leaving their baby?'

'You were never a monster. We regret not seeing the signs that you were distressed.'

'How could you know? I didn't even know what was happening. I know I wasn't a monster, it took me years to accept that, after a lot of counselling.'

'You look so happy. Dad and I said that before you came in,' said Anne.

'I am, Mum. It was terrible for so long. I am sorry to have put you both through that.'

'You have nothing to apologise for, Arianna, we loved you unconditionally, we are sorry we lost you for so long.'

'Gareth seems to make you happy,' Dad said.

They both listened intently to their daughter's life story after walking away at such a tender age.

'He does. He was very patient in the beginning when we met. Meeting Gareth at work as strangers, then becoming friends was a good thing. This was before any romance was ever kindled between us.

'I deliberately gave off the illusion of being a cold fish, so the staff avoided any contact if possible with me as the new start. Gareth, on the other hand, came up and asked to join me in the canteen. Initially, it was purely because of limited seating during lunches that I had to say okay. I was so battered and wounded. I made no eye contact. I always looked into the food on the tray.

Until he got the message and he left me alone. Ate his lunch, then off. On and on it went like this. Then one day, a nod and some eye contact followed. He was very patient, a truly lovely guy, completely trustworthy. A few days later, I smiled. He says it was so radiant. I said it was because he dropped his sandwich on the floor, then nearly fell over trying to retrieve it.

'That day I felt a shift when he departed, we smiled and that became our routine. This went on for a year. Until one day, Gareth asked if I would like to go to the pictures with him to see a music movie. It turned out to be an Oasis documentary. The documentary, while interesting, was also sad for me given it is your favourite band. I cried into one lonely tissue when they played "Don't Look Back in Anger".

'An awkward friendship was kindled, we started meeting out with work. He wanted to meet me twice in one week. I felt panic stricken and told him I couldn't meet too regularly. I insisted on that, I also know I had a very frightened look on my face. He knew something bad had happened and I was unwilling to trust anyone. After what Belinda did. Abandoned me in my hour of need, yet claimed she would always be there for me. That rejection changed the course of my life forever. I knew then that Gareth is a very kind man who was happy to be my friend and take things at my pace. As time went by, I found myself looking forward to our meetings. Gradually, I began to share a little, but never too much. I nearly flipped when he suggested we be friends on social media – it triggered such fear. He saw the colour drain from my face, noted this marked change in behaviour and said we could make plans at work. This genuine person became my confidant over time. I shared more about the past. I started with sharing about my very bad experience on social media.'

'Oh, love,' her parents said, unable to say anything else as the silent tears flowed listening to Arianna's difficult lonely road.

'I missed you both so much.'

'We missed you more than you will ever know. The whole family was broken hearted without you in our lives.'

'I am so sorry. So sorry,' said a now weeping Arianna.

'You have nothing to be sorry for, Arianna,' her parents said, reaching over and taking her hand. They were a circle again. The love flowed between them.

They gathered their composure.

'Keep going, love, tell us your story.'

'I don't need to hide my feelings anymore, I am so glad you are here with me now.'

'So are we, love.'

'The only one to ever know the whole story, Gareth, accepted it in its entirety. He respected the hard daily struggle caused by a woman called Belinda. It was a very hard recovery. In the beginning, I phoned the Samaritans many times, being lonely, sad or angry. I was always glad that there was someone on the end of the line who would listen. I once went and met a support worker. Then failed to keep appointments, I left the area, then never went back.

'I never had any desire to meet Toby. He was part of a different life, manipulated by an abusive adult. I worked out early on that survival was only possible by keeping that part of life locked inside and freezing out any emotions. Gareth, as the old cliché goes, started to literally melt my heart.'

***

The next day Oliver and Anne got the opportunity to let Arianna know about Denise and the vendetta. Gareth had taken the children out for a walk to give them time to talk. They talked at length about how someone could do that to a child. Arianna spoke of how stupid she was, but her parents reassured her that that wasn't the case. They spoke of Denise's demise.

'I'm pleased karma did its job, she will never do that to another person.'

'We would have told you about this supposed kiss, Arianna.'

'You knew everything about us, we really did not intend to hold anything back, I made my mistakes. You were always loved, Arianna.'

'I don't know why I never asked. Actually, I do. She made it sound sleazy, Dad.'

'I know. Mum took you and left me alone. Went to Nana's.'

'Oh, did you, Mum?'

'Yes. I made many mistakes, Arianna, but you were never one of them. My dad left us, I was devastated and blamed my mum. I was going through the teenage years. I loved your dad. I was angry one night and broke my arm on a tree.'

'NO! YOU! I can't imagine that would ever happen.'

'I did.'

'If only I had asked,' said Arianna.

'If only we had told you,' said Oliver and Anne.

Anne said, while looking at Oliver then Arianna, 'The kiss that day at university that Denise planted on Oliver's unavailable lips was not reciprocated. I do believe that bitch caught your dad unaware and kissed him. She had a crush on him when we were at school. Was rejected and let that fester like a poisonous sore for years. When we were young, Hazel, Caroline and I used to be friends with her, she was horrible then, but I thought maybe people can change.'

Even though the fire crackled away in the corner, they all involuntarily shuddered.

'How profoundly sad that our young girl, who had come from such a loving family, fell foul to that vindictive individual?' said Oliver.

'Why did I click the button? Why, instead of clicking a button in the early hours of one lonely morning, did I not climb out of bed, come down the stairs and ask you both?'

'You were young, you weren't to know,' said Anne.

'The web of deceit could have been so easily explained. Dismissed and forgotten,' said a forlorn Oliver. 'Instead, what happened was an appalling breach of trust. The judge said the rippling affects negatively impacted all our lives from then on. While that was true, it did nothing to reverse the situation for the people involved.'

'We know that better than anyone, we lived that life,' Anne added.

***

With the passing of time mother and daughter reconnected.

'I know you are busy with work, Dad; if that's the case why not come alone, Mum?'

Chapter Twenty-Six

Anne ran to catch the bus, her suitcase wheels rattling behind her. Her first trip ventured alone without the strength from her beloved husband by her side. There is now enough water under the bridge to ensure a peaceful visit.

'Return please.'

'Off somewhere nice?'

'To visit my daughter and family.'

'Lovely day for a trip.'

'Yes. Thanks,' said Anne.

The bus shuddered out of the station with the strong smell of fuel. The person across the aisle made eye contact with a smile, appearing desperate to chat, to make the journey go quicker. 'Hi.'

'Hi,' replied Anne, nervously reaching into the bag of snacks. She took out a treacle toffee and looked out the window away from the friendly face. She unwrapped the paper and popped it into her mouth. The sensation of flavours offered a sense of familiarity and comfort.

Feeling rude, she turned back to the friendly face who was now looking out the window. Anne settled back in her seat and continued looking at the passing scenery. The stickiness in the palm of her hand distracted her, requiring further exploration. Removing the small piece of toffee, Anne looked again at the palm of her hand, staring at it in awe. In her younger days, having had her palm read, who would ever have known just how accurate that elderly lady was in predicting Anne's future?

'You will have twin brothers.

'A child who …'

'What is it?' the young girl enquired with a mystified look and questionable expression. 'What else? Please tell me,' said the innocent young girl met with an unnerving gaze.

'Oh nothing, dear, you will find out,' was the reply. Anne muttered that the woman was a bitter old woman who envied her and the young life still to be lived.

The memories of this conversation so long ago came to her for some reason. As the bus went up hill and down dale, all the twists and turns of a bittersweet life started reeling through her mind, almost like a silent movie. It started with two young people, the strength of a family. The events of the past unravelled almost like a kitten playing, then becoming entwined in a multicoloured ball of wool. Each person's life, while separate, played a vital part in their family history.

The driver announced, with about thirty miles to go, that they would be arriving late at their destination. Some emergency situation at one of the bus depots accounting for the delay. Anne is quite content in her memories as she enjoys the last of the treacle toffees. A reminder of many childhood Halloween treats, this one particularly tantalises her tastebuds.

Something about the way the next young man looked as he sat down on the bus feels familiar to Anne. *Could this be how Toby would look as a man?*

Toby's path was difficult, always feeling incomplete. He hankered with thoughts of trying to trace his natural mother. His friends and family actively encouraged him. Unaware Arianna never wanted to be found.

Toby sat on the bus and wondered about his mum's appearance after all these years. He knew what age she'd be now. *I wonder if I will ever get to meet her. Do I have the same hair and eyes?*

Toby travelled about ten miles, got up and rang the bell. The young man then looked up the bus, Anne smiled, he smiled back and with that he was gone.

The bus arrived late. Anne's eyes filled with tears at the sight waiting for her. There on the platform was her daughter, Arianna, and her husband, Gareth.

'Hi, Mum. How was the journey?' said Arianna.

'Beautiful scenery, thanks. Sorry I'm late. How are you?' said Anne.

'It wasn't your fault, no need to apologise. We are all good,' said Arianna, leaning forward to hug her mum.

'Dad sends his love to you all.'

'Come on, you two,' Gareth joked. 'We can chat more at home, don't want to get stuck in traffic.'

Chapter Twenty-Seven

A nne spent hours walking during and after the trial. The constant mental chatter never left her. Distressed, Anne would arrive at either her mum's or Susan's house. Today, it was Morag who offered comfort.

'Do you think it's simply that what we ingest pre-birth interferes with the natural biology of the individual?'

'I don't know, Anne. Why? Come here, love,' said her mum with outstretched arms.

'I can't stop thinking about it. Do you think that Arianna was affected by me?'

'I don't know, Anne.'

'Do you think I could have stopped what happened to her?'

'No, Anne, you couldn't have,' said Morag with tears brimming in her eyes. Distraught to see Anne, and also Oliver, continually looking for a rational explanation for what happened to them. It was relentless, for years the whole family could not escape the void at every family function. It was awful. It was hard for them all to accept that Arianna had left Toby and neither would return home.

One day, as Anne visited Susan after work for tea (something they had started when Anne and Oliver moved out), Anne asked again about nature or nurture before Oliver arrived.

'I really don't know, darling. Look at Jason, was he a product of genetics? Or just took every environmental opportunity to the detriment of Oliver and me. We had a good life, so what happened? What do you think, is it nature or nurture?'

'Mmm yes,' said a forlorn Anne.

'I know it doesn't help you, Anne. Words fail me. That woman was evil, and I can never forgive what she did to us. With no reason whatsoever to target our family, choosing to execute an immature crush she had on Oliver. What kind of person carries that kind of hatred within them for that long?'

'Do you think that it's just possible that something in Denise lay dormant like some wild animal, waiting to be triggered by the environment to create that truly evil person? Or did she ingest more of the sweet 'golden liquid' of life, creating genetic distortion in all its complexity?'

'I don't know, darling, you're the one with the knowledge of the impact of nature on children's lives, Anne.'

'The way I see it,' she says affectionately, 'I always remember it by thinking nature is your genetic makeup, while I think of nurturing trees, so that becomes the environmental influences.'

'Very clever,' says Susan. 'I think I will remember that now, Anne. I can clearly see that's why you continue to do what you do. You are very good at that job of yours, Anne, you have found your niche. I know that every time we chat about your work. You light up and your passion is tangible.'

'Thank you, it was a hard road to travel with everything that happened.'

'I know, darling,' she says affectionately. 'Do you know how proud I am to call you my daughter-in-law?'

Anne pretended to ponder the question. 'Mm yes, I think I know,' she said, smiling at Susan who stepped forward to hug her, then they continued to prepare the tea together.

***

A few weeks later, Oliver came bounding through the door.

'I have some good news to share with you both,' he said with such excitement that the women looked from one to the other.

'Come on, spit it out,' said his wife, waving her hand in a rotated gesture.

'I had an email today at work. The family really enjoyed your recent visit …'

Anne, now bursting with excitement, said, 'Oliver, what is it?'

'Arianna and the family are going to come visit us here for the next visit. Can you believe that?'

They looked from one to the other with tears in their eyes. Anne then let out a scream of delight, got her phone from her handbag on the side, then called her mum to spread the good news.

A strong family unit, they were destabilised, they were broken. What this family will never forget is that, while evil overpowered them, they rose again, like a phoenix rising from the ashes. Maybe, just maybe, they'd be able to develop something akin to becoming a complete family once again.

Chapter Twenty-Eight

Music heals the soul. How true that was for this family. Each one of them had musical connections which burned deep inside. Hitting all their emotions as easily as the beat of whatever song was being sung at the time. Music can make you happy, it can make you sad. It can lift you up, it can bring you down.

'Did you know, lad,' Oliver's grandpa often said, 'on the 2nd October 1970 Donovan married his special girl Linda?'

'Yes, Grandpa, you tell me this every time we listen to "To Try for the Sun".' Fondly remembered from the many visits to their home, Oliver also loved the jovial banter and songs from both grandparents.

Susan particularly loved 'To Try for the Sun' which was sung with such gusto. As a youngster, Oliver remembered vividly his mum pointing upwards, as if towards the sun with outstretched arms and smiling, transferring that passion, that anything is possible if you really try, to the sun.

Oliver in turn passed that to their baby girl, and every time they heard that song on the radio, or when playing Donovan's album, little Arianna began to giggle and laughed as Oliver chased her round the living room, saying with affection, 'Stop running, you little munchkin, you will scratch my record.' Loving the chase, Arianna would stop, particularly when she was a toddler, wait, giggle, then try to run away.

Music can change when the mood is deflated, when that special person you shared sweet memories with is gone. The lyrics had gone from making him feel elated to feeling deflated. For years this song made him feel sad, wishing little Arianna was still in their lives.

The song came on in the car a few days later, and it made Oliver very happy, knowing Arianna would be visiting soon.

One Sunday, when the family had all gathered at Oliver and Anne's house, they were all sitting after lunch chatting when the phone rang. A new routine had been created, always around this time of day. Oliver answered, 'Hi, Arianna.'

The room now silent, they all listened intently. Phoning every Sunday, she gradually plucked up the courage to speak to each member of the family.

Her dad said, 'Is that "Try for the Sun" I hear playing?'

'Yes, it is, Dad,' came the reply at the other end of the line. His face shone with such happiness. Nodding, then nodding again, his daughter started to relay how this song was a favourite. It reminded her of happy times when she was a little girl, being chased by him and then being kissed and cuddled.

Then Morag came to the phone. 'Yes, I do still read my Mills and Boon books, you cheeky young scamp. Of course the story changes! I know, darling, you are right. I went to the library the other day and read my book. Then went for lunch in town and finished my book, very funny, no I cannot skip to the end as they all finish the same way,' said Morag with such happiness in her voice. They chatted a bit longer before Morag said, 'Bye, darling.' Turning to Anne, 'Arianna, wants to speak to you.'

Anne took the phone as Morag gently patted her arm and smiled. They chattered away on the phone about this and that, talking for some time. Oliver had the record player lid open, looking through their record collection. Finding the lost treasure, he put it on the turntable.

Over the following weeks a lovely new routine was established. This week the door opens, and in walked the twins with their respective families.

'We can't stay, Anne.'

'Good to see you all as always,' said Anne, kissing them all. They hadn't made it to dinner the week before.

'Oh, Ollie, put on Led Zeppelin "Stairway to Heaven".'

Oliver did, then they all played air guitar. There was laughter, there was chatter. 'To Try for the Sun' was played next. Mark and Michael looked at each other, then Anne told them the story Arianna relayed to Oliver of her memories.

'Oh that's great, Ollie,' said the twins, hugging him in a semi rugby tackle.

'Enough. What age are you?' Anne laughed.

'You know, big sis,' Mark said, lifting her high in the air.

'Ah put me down. Ollie, help me.'

'I'm not tackling them.' He laughed.

This family had had enough sadness to last a lifetime.

The following week, deep feelings of excitement and happiness were oozing from every window in number 4 Harmony Row.

The building looked the same from the outside, but the warmth had returned. The cold broken years, hopefully behind this family, ironically, brought back to life with the passing by of some ashes.

In actual fact, Denise's death did move their world forward. In a positive way, to the delight of one very special family, they had faced adversity and never gave up hope. The very fabric of this building knew that. The house now shone with such vibrancy that their story had to be felt not told.

That night, when watching *Working Girl*, Anne said, 'This is our Melanie Griffith moment, Oliver.'

'What do you mean?'

'If you flip that scene, Denise was that power-driven head teacher, who revelled in her ultimate power.'

'Mm, if you say so.'

The next family gathering was just before Arianna, Gareth and the children arrived to visit. If you lived two streets away, you would have heard them all sing so loudly to the record being played.

After the family arrived and the party was in full swing, the final rendition of the evening was of course Oasis singing '*Don't Look Back in Anger*'.

About the Author

Mairi has always had a keen interest in how children, young people and families develop over time and the issues affecting them since gaining an SNNEB qualification in early education and childcare in the early 1980s.

Mairi is a lecturer in a further education college and continues to thrive being with her students. They bring pleasure, happiness and a sense of fulfilment when doing a job she started when she was 19 years old. Mairi feels privileged to share her passion to promote theory to practice in her daily life.

Mairi is married, is a parent and is a delighted gran to their growing family. Family remains important to Mairi, with all of its trials and tribulations. With each passing year Mairi remains hopeful, from generation to generation, that the individual fabric woven within each family never becomes so thread bare that it breaks beyond repair.

Mairi enjoys writing during her holidays. Her first fictional novella, *Everything to Nothing and Back*, was written because of her keen interest in family structures, alongside a deep sadness for all women worldwide who had their babies forcibly taken from them. As an adoptee Mairi empathises with both sides of the story.

Losing Arianna is Mairi's second novel, which also focuses on children, young people and families and the contemporary topical issues affecting them.

You can contact Mairi on Facebook at facebook.com/mairispeirsauthor

Acknowledgements

To all the young people I have been privileged to meet and work with over the years from a nursery nurse to becoming a lecturer in a further education college. Each of you has touched my life and heart. Some good, some not so good. However overall, the good outweighs the bad.

Within my current job I see the impact for families of societal changes, and the impact of social media. I understand as someone who has grown up in a pencil and paper world. For some young people the harm and impact of social media has been catastrophic, yet I acknowledge the value of social media is undeniable for others.

The indelible footprints left on my heart by the young people I have met over the years has resulted in the creation of *Losing Arianna*. Bullying whether online or in person can destroy families. I believe firmly, this must continue to be challenged by each generation. Everyone has a voice, and to use it for the greater good, is the privilege of both young and old alike.

My thanks also to Indie Authors World.